A Boy Named Joe

M.O. Austin

Bloomington, IN Milton Keynes, UK

authorHOUSE®

AuthorHouse™
1663 Liberty Drive, Suite 200
Bloomington, IN 47403
www.authorhouse.com
Phone: 1-800-839-8640

AuthorHouse™ UK Ltd.
500 Avebury Boulevard
Central Milton Keynes, MK9 2BE
www.authorhouse.co.uk
Phone: 08001974150

First published by AuthorHouse   12/7/2006

ISBN: 978-1-4259-6217-3 (sc)

Printed in the United States of America
Bloomington, Indiana

This book is printed on acid-free paper.

BOOK 1:
THE ONE AND ONLY

PART 1: BIG JOE

Chapter 1: Meet Big Joe

This was the day everyone had long awaited. The new student was finally arriving. Everyone at Derlina Jackson High School loved it when new students arrived. It gave them fresh meat. You see, the people at this school; they loved to pick on the new kids. They would get them in trouble, suspended, and sometimes if they were feeling particularly obnoxious, expelled. Jackson had a reputation for housing the meanest, foulest, most rambunctious people in all of Maryland.

As the teenagers approached the school on the buses, they contemplated the ways they would harass the poor new kid. One by one, the students disembarked from the different buses, chatting excitedly about what the new kid would be like.

"If this one is anything like the last new kid, he's gonna be in for a wild ride," A student said.

"What do you think I should do first? Atomic wedgies or framing for stealing," another student said, who was about 5'4" with curly blonde hair. His nose was slightly crooked and he had a problem with halitosis, but no one ever questioned what he said because he was the toughest kid in the school. "Or maybe even, The Teacher's Chair Ride Of expulsion."

"Jack you are so evil."

"I know," he said. As they entered the building, everyone departed for their respective classes.

It was about 9:00 am when there was a knock at the door. The teacher, Mr. Jefferson, was nearly 6 feet 4 and bald with glasses. He had a beard that was rather short still, but well on the way to becoming the length of his chest. He answered the door. In stepped the new kid. He was about 6 feet 7 with braids in his hair. His nose was abnormally large with ears to match. His eyes were black as night and his lips were so big they were positively offensive. The new kid wore a black jumpsuit with black boots to match. His fingernails were so long and sharp, they appeared to be able to shred stone with a single swipe. The teacher looked a bit intimidated by this student's appearance but spoke out anyway.

"Class, this is Joseph Austin. I would like you to treat him a little more nicely than the last new student, which by the way, I hear should be getting out of that pesky sanitarium any day now," Mr. Jefferson finished. Joe looked at him and he let out a small yelp.

"*No one* is to call me Joseph. The name is Big Joe," He boomed across the room in a deep voice.

"Well don't you worry. We won't call you Joseph. We'll call you scum until you earn the right to have your name used," said the student Jack, who sat in the front row. Joe swelled with anger. His mouth opened and he let out a yell that shook the very walls of the building, picked up the student's desk, and hurled it out of the closed window. Glass was everywhere. Shards hit the floor and broke into tinier pieces. Other pieces flew through the air and cut people's arms and faces.

"Do you have something else to say?" snarled Joe in a menacing voice.

"Oh I'm scared!" Jack cried out mockingly and then began shrieking like a bat. "You're pathetic."

Joe grabbed Jack's chair from under him and proceeded to beat him over the head with it. It took the teacher and several other very strong students to pull Joe off of him. When Jack rose, his neck, nose, and ears were all bleeding.

"You think you're bad don't you? Well let's see how easily you can be broken," Jack threatened. Joe looked around, and not being able to see anything close he broke away from his captors and started beating Jack with his bare hands. This time, the school security guard had to be called in to escort Joe away.

In the principal's office, Joe sat in the chair looking as though he would like nothing more than to murder the woman staring across the table at him.

"What on earth were you thinking?" Principal Hanah asked him. Principal Hanah had red hair and a lot of make-up on. She was very petite and young-looking for her age (which everyone knew was really 67 despite her constant protests that she was only 39).

"I was thinking *'If this clown don't stop he's gon' have a big ole gunshot wound right through the chest.'*" Joe spoke truthfully. Principal Hanah looked appalled.

"You know that we're going to have to search you and your belongings after that statement. Right?", she added on at the end.

"You touch me… or my stuff… and I guarantee you're going to die by 8:00 Saturday morning. There'll be a lovely funeral by 12:30 that afternoon. I promise I'll bring flowers," Joe said.

"Young man, is that a threat?"

"No. Just consider it a word to the wise," Joe explained. Principal Hanah spoke again.

"We are going to have to give you a long term suspension for this." She said calmly

"For what?", Joe exclaimed.

"For threatening an administrator, doing bodily harm to another student, intimidating a teacher, and let's not forget that you're taller than all of us, which counts as major points against you. I mean, look at you and look at us. It's awful." She finished looking pleased.

"You can't suspend me you old hag! I was provoked on two of the three occasions. The teacher was a mistake. But that boy kept talking about me, and you were going to attempt to search me. You suspend me, and there's going to be hell to pay. I promise you. If you want to try me, be my guest." Joe said.

"I am the authority figure here and you shall do as I say. You should be threatened by me." She tried to convince him.

"Please. I've been more threatened by playing cards. Now, I will not be suspended, and you and your puny good for nothing students will show me the respect that I deserve. Understand?" Joe peered into her eyes.

"And just who do you think you are talking to? As I have already reminded you, I am the administrator here. You shall bow down before my excellence. You should be kissing my toes and begging me not to expel you." Principal Hanna said, puffing out her chest.

"Let's make a deal, the day I bow down to *you,* is the day that all hell freezes over. Now bring me up here for this stupidness again, and it won't be pretty."

"That's it. I'm calling the police," She said.

"Go ahead. Call them. I dare you."

"They'll haul you away."

"No they won't. Me and the police have a "buddy-buddy" relationship. I can have you hauled away though."

"I will not allow you to talk to me in this disrespectful manner." She said.

"You don't have a choice. I run this school now. And by the way, you look 70," He said smiling.

"You little-" she said, grabbing a letter opener and lunging at Joe. She stopped inches from his neck.

"Why'd you stop?"

"Because I have to protect you, you little shit," she mumbled, walking back to her desk.

"What was that?"

"Nothing!"

"You wanna know the real reason you stopped? Because you don't have the balls to kill a student." Joe said. And with that, he got up, and removed himself from the office.

Joe roamed the school for the next hour, taking in his new surroundings. He popped a few lockers, stole some CDs, CD players, and even some lunches. He inspected the bathrooms, which he wouldn't send his dog into. He peered inside a few of the classrooms, and saw kids peering back at him. When he felt as though his search was over, he stepped outside into the cool spring air. Joe went and set under the nearest tree and looked at the street. He sat there for about 10 minutes before the bell rung and signaled the end of the first class.

The rest of the day was pretty uneventful, Joe robbed some people, beat up the people who wouldn't let him rob them, and he even managed to scare the principal into retreating back into her office. The bus ride home however, was very interesting. Joe beat up 16 people in five minutes, without ever breaking a single sweat.

When he got home his mother and father were nowhere to be found. He searched their room and everywhere else, but they weren't there. Then, when he entered the kitchen, he found something that chilled his blood. There were two quite large puddles of blood on the new shiny white floor. And on the table there was a note that said simply

I've got them.

- You Know Who.

Chapter 2: The Notes

"You know who?" Joe said to himself. He went over to the other counter to get a paper towel and found another, longer note under the paper towels. Joe read this note several times. It took a while for the words to sink in.

Joe,

I figured you wouldn't be able to tell who the first note was from so I decided to leave another to help you out. I know that you remember me. You remember those two weeks in the hospital? The ones where you were so deep in a coma the man with the world's longest arms couldn't pull you out? Remember now? Of course you do. How couldn't you? Your parents aren't dead - **Yet**. But they will be if you show anyone this note. And I'll know if you do. I've already spent 10 years in prison because of your big fat mouth. If I have to spend anymore, your parents will meet their maker, in a not so pleasant way. I won't tell you exactly what I'll do. It's not time yet. Oh well, gotta go. Love ya lots!

-Heather

Joe crumpled up the note and threw it into the fireplace. He went upstairs to his room and punched a hole in the wall. He ripped the curtains, knocked over the lamps and broke his bed in half. He thought to himself, '*Not the safest way to vent anger, but it sure is the most effective.* Joe tore up everything that he could get his hands on. And then when he could tear up any more, he sat down on his parent's bed and fell directly to sleep.

A guard walks up to a cell. Inside the cell is a woman no older than 28. She has beautiful blue eyes, strawberry blond hair, and a rather large nose. She had a particularly evil look on her face. The guard opens the cell door.

"Such an ugly expression for such a pretty woman," He said with a smirk on his face. She looked up at him.

"I'm even more beautiful by light," She said seductively. As he fumbled with his flashlight, she grabbed a makeshift knife (which was really just an extremely sharp stone from out on the grounds). He opened the cell door and stepped inside. Heather grabbed the stone, jumped up and plunged it deep into his gut. He gasped out in pain, tears rolling down his cheeks. She twisted the stone around inside of him, and when he finally dropped top his knees, she pulled it out and left him for dead. After washing her hands, she set out (for some reason) past the open gates and began her journey towards freedom.

In her makeshift old apartment, things are exactly as she left them, including the picture of Joe on the wall. She looked at the stone and threw it at the picture. When the stone made impact, it split Joe's face in half. She smiled and said to herself,

"Now it's time for the fun to begin."

Joe woke , startled, sweat dripping down his face. He had never had a dream like that before, and to make matters worse, somewhere during the course of the dream he peed on himself. He looked down at the leg of his pants, which was now wet and matted to the hairs on his leg. He looked back onto his parent's bed, which now held sheets with a foul smelling yellow liquid on it. Joe got up and washed the sheets, and then took a shower and flipped his parent's mattress. Once the mattress was flipped, he looked over at the alarm clock, which now read 10:32. Feeling both hungry and a little sick, Joe went downstairs into the refrigerator to hopefully find something to make for dinner. Instead, he found yet another note. This one longer than the first two. He read it over, feeling his anger surge up again.

Hello again Joseph,

Did you have a nice nap? I bet you did. I looked in through the window and saw you tossing and turning, were you having a bad dream little Joey? Is that it? Was baby Joey having a bad dream?? Well get over you little baby! If you think whatever you dreamed about was scary, try spending 10 years in prison. Try not being sure if you're going to be caught in a fight and get killed by weight training equipment. Now that's something to have a nightmare about. Any way, I just thought that you should know that the games are on. You're gonna die for what you did. I didn't much like prison Joe. So what I'm gonna do is simple. I'm gonna kill you, gut you, and leave the country. Doesn't that sound like fun? You do anything you want to protect yourself, but remember if you go to the police your parents are dead. I've even left you something that might help protect you. Well, I hear you shuffling around upstairs so I gotta go. Check behind the milk.

-Heather

Joe crumpled the note again, and once again tossed it into the burning fireplace. He pulled the milk out of the fridge and set it on the counter. When he turned back around he saw two items. The first that he picked up looked like a wooden rod with a handle. The wood was long and smooth and strangely enough, was reddish brown. It was at least 14 inches with words carved into the side of it. It said, *Carrez Mahset Littstella.* The handle, at first was uncomfortable in Joe's hand, but after a moment conformed to fit his grip perfectly. The second item was a beautiful golden coin. On it there was a great "**I**", surrounded by four letters. They were: **P D F H.** He picked up the coin and instantly felt a rush of power. Though nothing happened. He inspected the coin a little more closely. It was indeed solid gold and quite heavy. At that moment, a thought occurred to him. He had always seen things like this in movies. He looked at the wooden rod, and inspected the words on the side very closely.

"*Carrez Mahset Littstella!*", he bellowed. Suddenly, the coin began glowing violently and shaking in Joe's hand. A moment later, a light shot out of the coin and directly into the fireplace and the fire was extinguished. In its place was a bluish portal. Of course, curiosity got the best of Joe and he stepped forward. He looked deep into the portal, but could see nothing on the other side. Deciding to test before he went any further, Joe plunged his hand into the portal. Suddenly, the greatest feeling of warmth that Joe had ever felt in his life overtook him. Not being able to handle it any more, Joe jumped inside. He felt himself spinning around violently and vomiting all over himself. After 10 seconds of this, Joe stopped spinning and hit a very hard surface. Afraid of what he might see, he reluctantly opened his eyes.

Chapter 3: The Illurian Hotel

As Joe slowly opened his eyes, all he saw was black. *Damn it! The fall made me blind,* he thought to himself. When his eyes were completely open he tried to look around. Then he realized he wasn't blind, because he saw a stand, with a large black shining stone upon it. There was a single light shining on the stone. As a matter of fact, it was the only light in the room. Joe pulled himself to his feet and walked over to the stone. He looked into it longingly, wishing that he knew where exactly where he was. Suddenly another light began shining in the stone. This light was from somewhere else. The light reflected from the stone and into his hand. A bright green ball of energy was shining within his hand. Out of curiosity, Joe touched the stone with the light. The stone glowed and it, along with its stand, sank into the floor. At that moment, the room lit up and Joe finally got a chance to see his surroundings.

Joe was standing in the lobby of a magnificent building. The floors were a checkered marble and there were columns all over the walls large enough for someone to hide. Above Joe was the most extravagant chandelier he had ever seen in his life. It was made of pure crystal and diamonds and had 4 levels. In front of him were stairs. The stairs were golden with rubies and sapphires embedded within them. Joe turned around and behind him stood a door 20 feet high with Silver knobs and all kinds of diamonds placed all around.

Feeling adventurous, Joe explored the lobby. There were many doors, but all of them were locked. When his search was over, he turned back towards the steps and saw something that he had not seen at first - a great sign, one foot high, that said in crystal letters:

The Illurian Hotel.

Before Joe climbed the stairs to the first floor, he went back and got the wooden rod and coin, and pocketed them, then went up the stairs. When Joe got to the first floor, there was a door to the left and a door to the right. Neither door had any label so he just entered the one on the left first.

In this room Joe nearly had heart failure at first glance. In front of him was the oddest assortment of creatures he had ever seen in his life. There were chairs walking around on their legs, lizard looking things making drinks, and worse, the lizard looked as though he was having a highly interesting conversation with the glass he was now filling with a red lava-like substance. What's even worse, the cup was talking back to it. The lizard looked up.

"Ahhh. Welcome to the Illurian hotel's Bar Of Mystery," It said.

"Yes. You never know what you'll get. Ow ow OW! Watch it with the Lava whiskey!" The glass said in a squeaky voice.

"The What?" Joe asked.

"Lava Whiskey," The lizard said. "The hottest substance in *any* dimension. Hot enough to burn a whole through 5,627 layers of steel, and keep on burning. Go on. Have a glass."

"No, No that's ok," Joe said.

"Have a glass," The glass said. "Have me."

Joe didn't want to offend these obviously mutated creatures, so he went over and plopped down on a stool. He heard muffled yelling and felt hot breath on his behind. He got up.

"Watch who you're plopping down on - you Neanderthal! Do you have any idea how easily you could have broken me? I'm a very fragile creature. No one even knows I'm around," The stool said.

"Hey Lenny," The glass said. "I thought you were on vacation."

"See what I mean?" The stool asked and walked away. Joe walked to another stool, and this time made sure that it didn't have a face before he sat down. The Lizard handed Joe the glass.

"Be careful though. The particles can sometimes stick to your gums," the lizard told him. Joe nodded and downed the glass. Big mistake. This was absolutely the hottest thing that had ever encountered before. He opened his mouth to ask for water but the words didn't come out. Fire did. The fire shot a whole through the wall and outside into the night. The lizard handed Joe a glass that contained a blueish substance. Joe didn't care what it was, he just downed it all. His mouth instantly froze, which was a nice sensation. But the rest of his insides froze as well. He didn't complain about this, he just figured that the ice would melt after a while.

Joe decided that he should get away from the bar and check out the rest of the room. There was a vase chatting with the flowers that it held, and a hunk of wood chasing a chair around the room. Joe couldn't handle it anymore. He ran from the room and slammed the door shut behind him.

Joe took a minute to catch his breath and wondered whether or not he should go into the other room. He decided that he would. He placed his hand on the knob, took a huge breath and pushed the door open.

This room was much tamer than the other one. It appeared to be a lounge of some sort. There were plush chairs seated in front of a large stage. On the stage there were harder chairs, and a few tables, and even instruments. It looked as though someone was preparing to perform there. The chairs looked quite inviting so Joe went and took as seat in one of them.

It was as though he was hurled through time. When the wind and the feeling of sickness subsided, Joe opened his eyes. There was no difference except that now, there were people on the stage. There was a woman dressed in a very blue outfit singing a song in a different language. The song was quite slow and the dancers surrounding the woman appeared to be doing a ballet. Behind the stage, Joe read the name of this room:

The Mystic Thread.

He looked around the room and everything was different. There were people all around him dressed in very strange clothing. They were clapping and snapping with the beat of the music, and some were even up and slow dancing. There were lights issuing from the ceiling and shining on both the people on stage, and the people in the audience. The woman on stage hit a particularly high note and then the song stopped. A faster song then began and the people around him started dancing like there was no tomorrow. For some reason, Joe felt himself falling into a deep sleep and fought to keep his eyes open. Finally he summoned enough strength to hoist himself out of the chair. As soon as he was standing straight up, the woman and her dancers were gone. Joe looked around the room and everyone was gone. It was just a room again.

Joe left this room and went farther upstairs to the second floor. Again there were two doors. This time, Joe picked the one on the right first. He entered the room and saw nothing but a black marble floor, a stage, and a very large disco ball hanging from the ceiling. Joe saw a light switch next to him. When he flipped it on, a change happened.

Joe looked up and there were now people dancing around the room in magnificent gowns and tuxedos. The women had their hair teased up into large towering masses. Joe wondered how they were able to fit though the door. The men had on top hats that Joe himself would have described as mini leaning towers of Pisa. There was very loud classical music playing, but the people were not dancing to this. Each couple had on a conjoined set of earphones and was dancing to whatever music was coming from them. Again, on the wall just behind the stage was the name of the room:

The Ballroom

The name was written in glowing white letters. Joe flipped the switch again and everything vanished before his eyes. Joe exited the room and went across the hall.

This next room was unlike any of the others. It was covered from top to bottom in the most beautiful and exotic plants that Joe had ever seen. There was a gigantic piano in the middle of the room. Inscribed on the top of the piano in glowing green letters was the name of this fragrant room:

The Mystical Garden

was the most beautiful thing Joe had ever seen in his life. It had every type of flower in the world inside of it. There were even flowers that Joe had never seen in books or on the Internet. Joe sat down in front of the piano and it began to play itself. It played a wonderful tune that Joe had never heard before. He expected a woman to suddenly appear on the piano, but no one came. After a minute Joe got up and headed towards the door. Suddenly he heard singing. He turned around and saw a woman in a beautiful green and blue gown. She beckoned Joe back towards the piano. And he obeyed. Upon his arrival at the piano, she stopped singing. She put her hand out and Joe took it. He was lifted off his feet and began to spin around. When his feet touched the ground again, everything was glowing. The flowers and plants had grown and the smell was even more enticing than before. Joe looked around and saw fairies flying around. Each time one touched down on a flower it grew and became more beautiful. One fairy came close to Joe's face and touched his nose. It was like nothing he had ever felt before. A warmness filled his very soul and every angry feeling that he had melted away. The fairy couldn't have been any bigger than Joe's thumb. None of them could have been. But they possessed such power. Joe looked at the woman on the piano, then looked back at the fairy. The creature smiled and then flew away. Jumping on flowers as it went. He turned back to the woman and took her hand once more. Once again he was lifted from the ground and began to twirl through the sky. He landed back in the normal garden and the woman vanished. Joe smiled, but then felt his angry feelings returning so he turned to the door and left.

On the third floor there was only one door. This door led to a very long hallway. Filled with thousands of bedrooms. Joe didn't have nearly enough strength to search them all, so he just shut the door and moved farther up the stairs.

The final floor had two doors. There was one to Joe's right, and one directly in front of him. The door to his right was black and had white writing inscribed upon it:

The Shadow Zone.

Joe did not want to explore this room, but he felt as though he must. So he opened the door, and right away he wished that he hadn't. Shadows poured from the room and surrounded Joe. He couldn't see anything but black. And he could feel the coldness of the shadows all around him. He quickly became afraid and longed to be out. He then felt rushing wind and saw the shadows rushing past him and back into their confinement, the door slamming shut behind them.

The final door had a piece of board over it, though it was not closed off. On the door there was black writing. The sign said simply

Rooftop. Enter at you own risk.

Joe was feeling risky so he opened the door and ascended the final flight of stairs. When he reached the roof, he was hit with a burst of cool air. He went over to the ledge and peered out. Two miles seemed to be encased in glass. But Joe could see just beyond the glass, and he didn't like what he saw. There were dragons and giants and all sorts of horrible creatures ravaging the land. There were buildings on fire, forests burned down and other buildings collapsing by the second. The closest creature was a 30-foot tall dragon. The dragon had black scales and fiery red eyes. Joe guessed that this creature was responsible for most of the destruction. Wishing that he could help them, Joe closed his eyes when he realized that he couldn't. When he opened his eyes, Joe saw that a crystal walkway had appeared in front of him. He stepped out onto the walkway and slid out. As he neared the glass he saw that a hole had appeared. The closer he got the faster he went. Joe had the most odd feelings as he slid along. There were feelings of happiness and then great sorrow. There were feelings of love and then lust for an unknown figure. And when he was on 12 feet away Joe slipped, and plunged head first into the darkness below.

Chapter 4: Aronus

Joe fell softly onto his softer than usual bed, which somehow had been completely repaired. Everything was normal again. His room was spotless, as though nothing had ever happened. There was only one difference; his pillow now had **The Illurian Hotel** stitched into it. As soon as Joe laid his head down he fell into a deep sleep.

That night, Joe dreamed of everything that he had seen in that glorious Hotel. The garden, and the thread, and the ballroom. But there was one thing that stood out in particular, the roof. The things that he had seen on the other side of that glass. What if there were people living in those buildings? When he awoke the next morning he figured that it was all a dream.

Joe quickly dressed and set off for school, completely disregarding his parents' absence and the now dry pool of blood in the kitchen floor. At school everything was different. People literally bent over backwards to get themselves out of Joe's way. The teachers were particularly nice to him and even the principal gave him her own lunch money. Joe enjoyed the special treatment but doubted that his beat down on Jack yesterday had anything at all to do with it. It wasn't until locker break that he found out exactly what was going on. He overheard two gossiping girls talking to each other.

"Joe who," One girl gasped.

"Joe Austin," The other girl said.

"Jackie, don't lie to me."

"I'm not Jill," Jackie said.

"You're serious? He really killed his parents," Jill exclaimed.

"Yes. Their blood is like all over the kitchen floor."

"How do you know," Jill asked.

"Apparently, Jack went over to his house yesterday to beat him, and he saw their bodies in the middle of the floor. And then, Joe dragging them out of the house," Jackie said. Jill asked,

"Did he see his face?"

"No. He had on a hood," Jackie told her. Joe slammed the locker shut and both Jill and Jackie jumped.

"Who did you say told you that?" Joe asked menacingly. Jill fainted and Jackie took off up the hall at a dash.

Joe went back to class boiling with anger. In the middle of an extremely tedious lecture on the civil war, Joe looked down at his book and saw something odd. There was a *very* mini man, standing between in the crease between the pages. This man was very fat with a dark blue circle around his eye, that same eyelash a foot long, and a top hat. The man's clothes were obviously several sizes too small for him. His clothes as well as his top hat were a violent shade of green. He spoke in a voice that filled Joe's head.

"Hey there! Why so glum chum? Is life getting you down? Well sir why on earth did you come back here? You could have had everything you ever wanted if only you had stayed at my wonderful hotel!" Joe looked around. Obviously no one else heard it because they were still listening to the teacher drone on. Joe looked back down very confused. "Don't you look at me like that! I'll slap you so hard you'll still feel it in a year. Do you want to come back or not?" Joe nodded. "Then say the spell. Come back. We can always use new faces." He laughed and sank into the crease. Joe remembered the rod and the coin. Both of which were in his locker. He got up and left the classroom without a word to anyone.

Once at his locker he retrieved both items and walked off into the bathroom. He held the coin in his hand and said,

"*Carrez Mahset Littstella*!" Again, the coin began glowing and shaking violently in Joe's hand. Only this time, when the coin opened the portal it was in the entrance to one of the stalls. Joe stepped in and once again was spinning more quickly than he had wished to a place that he knew nothing about. He was going back to The Illurian Hotel.

He landed again in the middle of the lobby, but this time the lights were already on. Also the man from Joe's book was standing near the stairs.

"Well it took you long enough," He said.

"Who are you," Joe asked the stranger.

"The name's Aronus. I'm the owner of this beautiful establishment," He said smiling.

"You're really the owner of this place," Joe asked.

"Why of course. This wonderful hotel has been in my family for generations. Thousands of years."

"If this is a hotel then where are all of the guests," Joe inquired.

"In their rooms of course. I saw you exploring the building last night. What did you think?" Aronus asked him.

"I think it's great. But..."

"Look boy, I know why you're here. You want to find your parents. While they're not in this building, they are in this dimension. They're just on the other side of the glass." Joe remembered the glass. Everything that he had seen beyond it had been so horrible. How could his parents end up over there?

"Heather sent you to the wrong place. You were supposed to end up on her side of the glass. Not here." Aronus said, reading his mind.

"How do you know about Heather?" Joe asked, confused. "Oh please! She's been causing trouble here for years. Ever since some snot nosed kid got her locked up when she was 18. The only thing is, she somehow tapped into the dark aspect of the hotel. That's how she created the barrier between this world and hers. On this side there's all the good. On here side though, there's every vile and evil thing you could possibly imagine. She's got the ancient demons on her side. The ones that came before everything else. You know, the dinosaurs. She's got dragons and giants and things that you can't possibly imagine over there. We've been trying to beat her for the longest time. But none of us can get past the glass. You're the only one that's even gotten off of the rooftop and close to it. When I saw that I knew. I knew that you're the one," Aronus said.

"Do you honestly expect me to believe that bull? There's no such thing as demons. There's no such thing as dragons. There's no such thing as creatures that go bump in the night," Joe said.

"Well then how do you explain what you saw last night?"

"I was tired. When people are tired they start to see things."

"You were not seeing things! All of it was real," Aronus said, offended that Joe didn't believe him.

"Look I don't know what you're playing, but keep me out of it. All I want is to find my parents," Joe said, his temper rising.

"You want to see your parents, huh? Then just look at this!" Aronus waved his hand and a giant screen appeared right in front of the stairs. The edge of the screen was flaked in gold, silver, and red. Aronus waved his hand again and an image popped up.

There were two people chained on a wall, one was a man wearing ridiculously thick glasses. He had a pointed nose and bright green eyes, which seemed to be magnified 100 times by his glasses. The other was a woman. She had beautiful blonde hair and blue eyes. She even had a petite nose, but she had "Dumbo-like" ears. Both were under guard by a positively evil looking dragon. It had two seven inch horns, bright red eyes, a snout, markings all around his eyes, and a nose large enough to fit a small group gathering into.

Joe stood rooted to the spot, a horrified look on his face. He wouldn't care if the two people were anyone else, but these were his mother and father!

Chapter 5: The New Powers

Joe stared at the screen, unable to believe what he was seeing. He watched as a rat scuttled into the room, was burned to a crisp by the dragon's fire breath and was then devoured in one chomp. Aronus waved his hand again and the screen disappeared.

"Those...those people... they're my parents." Joe said, feeling tears well in his eyes for the first time.

"I know. That's why you have to stop her. She has your parents, and if she ever figures out a way to do it, she's going to unleash that army that she's building on this and every other world", Aronus said.

"What... what do I have to do to stop her?" Joe asked, his voice shaking.

"Do what you do best. Inflict pain." Aronus said.

"But I don't know if I can do that. It's her fault I'm so angry all the time."

"Then take it out on her. Do back to her whatever she did to you to get you this angry." Aronus explained.

"I don't know..."

"Look, I'll make it easy for you. I'll give you lessons in the most powerful magic in the universe."

"Magic isn't real!!" Joe shouted.

"Yes it bloody well is! What do you think created this magnificent dwelling? Erosion? Now listen here young man. Magic is just as real as you and me! You don't have to believe it if you don't want to, but if you want to save your parents you'll listen to me." Aronus shouted back at him, obviously offended by Joe's disbelief.

"You're crazy. That's the only possible explanation. I've fallen asleep and now I'm having a dream about a guy who wears clothes way too small for him. That came out a lot more disturbingly than I intended." Joe said.

"Would you like to see some magic Joe?" Aronus asked. "Sure. Why not?" Joe said. Aronus muttered,

"*Te invoc Te, Beljoxas siri.*" The chandelier overhead began shaking dangerously, and then began emitting a bright blue light that surrounded Joe. He went into a sort of a trance for the next 10 minutes, in which Aronus did everything from dusting the stairs to filing his eyelash. When the light died out, Joe's eyes glittered with something that had not been there before. Real power.

"Well it's about time!" Aronus spat. "You must really be a complicated young child."

"W-What did you do to me?" Joe asked. "I unlocked the power within you. Everyone has some kind of power inside, they're just too jaded, stupid, or religious to see it. Those religious types think that any type of magic is wrong. It's not. It's not the magic that's wrong, or sinful, it's what some people decide to do with it. And they're afraid that if they have anything to do with magic they'll be corrupted or something. It's sickening", Aronus explained. "There's no such thing as magic!" Joe spat him.

"Oh yeah. Picture it: Your parents being tortured in that hell dimension out there and there's nothing that you can do about it. Heather's just out there having herself a good ole laugh. And there's nothing you-"

"Just **SHUT UP!**" Joe shouted and a near by vase exploded.

"There it is. Your first power. It's linked to your anger." Aronus said, pleased.

"What do you mean first?" Joe questioned.

"You must have more, you're still young."

"I don't want this! I don't want anything to do with magic! It only leads to bad things." Joe snapped at Aronus, his temperature rising.

"Well how do you think you got here? Huh? By clicking your heels together and saying 'there's no place like the Illurian hotel'? You really are stupid. Magic is everywhere; you just have to be open-minded enough to see it. What do you think is guarding your parents?" Aronus asked him.

"A dragon."

"Which is only found in the *magical* world. The evil one anyway..." Aronus trailed off.

"Magic is magic. Plain and simple, black and white."

"There is nothing black and white! About anything! Just look around you, you're in a place filled with color and light. If you use it properly, magic can be the most beautiful thing in the universe. If you use it improperly, then it could lead to disaster and heartache. Please. You have to believe me. The fate of all worlds rests upon you", Aronus pleaded.

"I'll save everyone the trouble, I won't use it at all." Joe said and stormed away.

"Get back here you stupid child!"

Joe stomped up to the door and tried to open it, but it wouldn't budge. He then turned around and ran up the stairs. He could still hear Aronus shouting at him to come back, but he did not listen. He searched the hotel top to bottom but found no exit. There was only one way out, the roof.

Joe ran onto the roof and jumped straight off. *'I'm going home'*, he thought to himself, but instead of landing in his bed he landed back in the lobby of the hotel. He looked around and now saw a door labeled

Dungeons.

He decided to take his chances and ran downstairs. At the bottom of the stairs, Joe saw two passages, but just to his right he saw another door, this time labeled

The "Real" World

Joe opened the door and was instantly pulled inside.

Joe found himself spinning around and around and around. He began to get dizzy and shut his eyes. After a minute he hit a soft surface. He opened his eyes and looked around, and to his delight, he was back in his room. Joe laid down and fell immediately to sleep.

Chapter 6: The Diviantoids

When Joe arrived at school the next morning, he was pissed and he wasn't taking any body's crap. As he walked to class he saw that a kissing couple was in his way. He didn't even bother asking them to move, or even going around them. When he got to them he simply pushed them both into lockers at opposite ends of the hallway and continued walking without ever stopping. Even the teachers sensed that there was a problem with Joe; they didn't even bother trying to get him to participate. When he saw a guy looking back and sneering at him, once the boy had turned around, he threw a pen at the back of his head. The boy had to go to the nurse with the pencil still sticking out of the back of his head.

After class was over, Joe went outside and sat down under a tree and waited for his next class to start. When a 9th grade boy asked him to scoot over so that he could share the shade, Joe stood up, grabbed the boy by the collar, and punched him in the nose before tossing him out in the street. When his watch beeped signaling the start of his next class, Joe got up and made his way into the building towards his science class.

After 30 minutes of listening to the teacher talk about cleaning fluids, he was allowed to do what he wanted to do - experiment. The assignment was to try to improve upon the cleaning fluids that were sold in stores. Joe got a large pot and heated it over his fire. Once the pot smelled as though it were ready to melt from the heat, Joe added an entire bottle of Clorox. Joe began adding random things that he had no idea what really to do with them all. He added some blue liquids, and some red ones, and yellow, and green, and purple, and clear. Finally, he spit in the pot and it began to bubble.

"I'm finished." He called to his teacher. The teacher walked over and looked at Joe's concoction, which had gone from clear to a lavaish color and texture.

"What is this?" The teacher asked looking quite puzzled. "My cleaning fluid." Joe said.

"Well then let us test it. If it properly cleans an object of your choosing, you pass. If it doesn't clean it you get a triple zero."

"Fine, whatever." Joe said as he motioned for a nearby boy to come over. When the boy approached Joe he picked up a stool and bashed him in the nose with it.

Blood streamed from the boy's nose and all over his clean white tee shirt.

"Mr. Austin! Exactly what do you think you're doing?", the teacher shouted at Joe.

"Chill out you old fool. Just watch." Joe said pulling the shirt off the boy and tossing it into the pot, ignoring the teacher's threats to have him hauled away. Joe grabbed a large metal object and dipped it into the pot to retrieve the shirt.

When Joe pulled the shirt out it looked good as new. It was completely white again, and to everyone's amazement, dry. Everyone applauded as the teacher marked down an A on his grade sheet. Joe was excused from class early and went back to his tree. He didn't have any more classes until 2:15. It was 1:00. *It is so good being a senior.* Joe thought to himself as he drifted off to sleep.

Joe was awakened by a sickeningly strong whiff of perfume. He nearly gagged, the smell was so strong. When he opened his eyes he found himself face to face with none other than Principal Hanah.

"Exactly who do you think you are young man?" she asked, spraying him with spit.

"I know who I am. Do you know who you are?" Joe asked her. She lifted him up by his collar and slammed him into the tree. She lifted him so high that his feet were dangling an inch off of the floor.

"Now listen here you little shit-head. I told you once before that I am the administrator here. Being the administrator I demand respect! And if you continue to talk to me in the manner that you have been, I am going to rip you a new one. Do you understand me?" Joe didn't speak. "I said do you UNDERSTAND me?" She spat, lifting him a little higher up.

"Yes!" He said to her with spite in his voice. She lowered him onto his feet.

"Now, I've come down here to talk to you about the way that you behaved in science class. Now come with me to my office." She said and began walking. Joe followed behind her.

As they neared the science classroom there was a flash of green light and the teacher came soaring out of the room and slammed into a wall.

"Mr. Willis!" Principal Hanah shrieked and ran to his aid. Just then Joe saw a hooded figure glide out of the room and several others behind it. These things had on stormy gray and white hooded robes. Even under their hoods, Joe could just make out its face. All of these creatures had incredibly grotesque faces, and horribly distorted features. Their faces had giant lumps growing out of both sides of it, large eyes devoid of pupils, and ritualistic markings all around their faces. Their mouths were oddly crooked and seemed frozen into a smile. Their noses bulging disgustingly from the rest of their faces, their ears were almost non-existent, and their eyes were nothing but swirling white vortexes.

One of them dived at Joe but just missed him. He took this as his cue to run. Joe ran through the school and found himself in the cafeteria. When he turned back around he saw three of them gliding at him. He ran and dived behind the lunch counter figuring that they would leave if they heard nothing. But then he heard something. A high-pitched blood-curdling scream that came from near the door. Joe peeked over the counter and saw those awful creatures with the boy he had hit with the stool with earlier. One was holding him by his neck, using a nasty black and blue swollen hand. As soon as the boy looked down at the creature he began screaming and writhing trying to get free. He opened his mouth to scream again, but nothing came out. Well, not a voice anyway. Instead, a yellowish mist came from the boy's mouth and flew into the creature's eye. The boy suddenly looked as though all of the joy in the world was gone. He looked as though he were highly depressed. The thing dropped him and glided from the room. Joe jumped from behind the counter and followed it. Joe reached the science room but the things were nowhere to be found. Joe heard the teacher stutter from by the opposite wall.

"T-T-Those t-t-t-t-things! They c-c-c-came from y-y-y-y-y-your pot!" Joe looked in the room at his pot, which was sitting on the table. He had an idea.

Joe rushed inside the room and grabbed a beaker filled with liquid nitrogen. He ran over to his pot and poured the nitrogen in. His cleaning fluid froze instantly. Joe then tipped the pot over and the now frozen contents Shattered on the floor. There was a loud rumbling, and then a dozen of those horrible creatures came swarming into the classroom. They formed a giant tornado around the biggest piece of frozen fluid, and were sucked inside by an invisible force. When the last of them was gone, Joe let out a giant sigh of relief. But his now calm nature lasted for only a few seconds. For once the students had gotten quiet and stopped screaming, a gunshot rang out through the silence.

Chapter 7: The Barrier Between The Worlds

Everyone stood rooted to their spots as Principal Hanah went to check and see what had happened. She came back looking very grim.

"Everyone outside." She said quietly. Once everyone was assembled outside Principal Hanah began to speak. "It is my extreme displeasure to have to tell you that your classmate, Jerry Hilkos, has killed himself", she said. Several girls burst into fits of tears. A few of the boys gasped. But Joe just stood there. He had seen what those creatures did to him and he just ran right past him instead of stopping to see if he was ok.

"I need to be excused please." Joe managed to say, even though he didn't know how.

"Yes, yes of course." Principal Hanah said, and Joe headed off toward the bathrooms.

He drew (what he now called) the Illurian coin from his pocket and said the magic words.

"Carrez Mahset Littstella!", he cried. Once again the coin began to glow and opened the portal to The Illurian Hotel. He stepped inside and prepared for the rapid spinning once again. But it didn't come. He just dropped through what he assumed was the floor of the portal and landed neatly in the lobby of the hotel.

Aronus was sitting on the stairs, looking as though he knew this moment was coming.

"I knew you'd be back." He said smugly.

"What did you do?" Joe asked him.

"I didn't do anything. You did."

"What are you talking about?" Joe asked, clearly puzzled.

"You left the door open. And what's worse, you were careless with your potion making!" Aronus' voice began to rise.

"Potion... What are you talking about?"

"I put the ingredients in your head while you were under the light. While you were in science you were supposed to make a potion that would enable you to pass between the barrier without that pesky spell. But you had to spit in it. The acid in you saliva is what turned it into lava." Joe thought of the lava whiskey. It wasn't his fault. But he continued listening to Aronus' ramblings. "Instead of making a way for you to pass between the barrier unharmed, you burned the whole thing down!" Aronus shouted

"What barrier? What are you talking about?" Joe asked.

"THE BARRIER BETWEEN THE WORLDS!" Aronus shouted.

"Stop yelling at me!" Joe said through clenched teeth.

"Then stop being an idiot! Any sane person knows that there's an invisible barrier separating all of the different worlds and dimensions. Or *was* one anyway. Before you burned it down. Don't you roll your eyes at me. You obviously do not understand the seriousness of what you have done. The worlds, they were meant to stay separated. There are things on some worlds that some were meant to never handle. Like that." He said, pointing over Joe's shoulder.

Joe turned to see one of the creatures from the school gliding in through the **closed** door. Aronus pointed his finger at it and shouted,

"*Petrinolious!*" The creature literally froze on the spot. Within a second, a thick sheet of ice covered the thing. Then it shattered into a million tiny pieces.

"What was that?!" Joe asked.

"Diviantoid. It's an elite species of... well to tell the truth I'm not sure what they are. All I know is that they're bad news. They literally suck the happiness right out of people. They feed on it I guess. Anyway, once all happiness is gone, the person is in a deep despair and is eventually driven to suicide." Aronus said.

"How long does that normally take?" Joe asked.

"About a month. But that's only if you're used to them. If it's your first time encountering them it could be-"

"A few minutes?" Joe cut him off.

"Yes. But how did you-"

"They attacked my school. I watched them suck the happiness out of this kid named Jerry." Joe said.

"Why didn't you do anything to stop them?" Aronus asked. "I didn't know how. I had never seen them before. The worst part of it was the screaming. He was so afraid. And :I sat there, knowing that there was nothing I could do about it. That if I went out there that I'd end up like that too." Joe said, his voice beginning to break.

"Yeah I know. I had a run-in with them when I was little. My parents took me too a planet that they just happened to be on. My dad died screaming, and there was nothing we can do about it. Instead of just taking his happiness, they took him. And there was nothing left but a shell." Aronus said with tears beginning to well up in his eyes.

"Look, we can't mourn the dead. Not right now. Show me where this barrier was." Joe said.

"Oh so you believe now? Aronus asked him.

"Do I have much of a choice? I mean, a race of things I've never even heard of just attacked my school."

"Ok. I'll show you were it was."

They walked up the stairs and stopped in front of

The Shadow Zone.

"I don't like this place." Joe said.

"Oh come on! You never even went in," Aronus said. "Quit being such a baby!"

"I'm not being a baby. I opened the door and was completely engulfed by shadows. What does this room do?" He asked.

"It shows you what you want to see. It gives you what you want to have. It's basically the nerve center of the whole fantasy aspect of the hotel. Now what you have to do is, as soon as the shadows surround you think of how much you want to see the barrier." Aronus explained.

"Ok." Joe said as Aronus wrenched the door open and shadows engulfed him. He focused on how much he wanted to see the barrier. He felt himself losing grip with reality. He felt like he was spiraling down a flight of stairs.

Suddenly he stopped and the shadows cleared away. He looked around him. It was like he had completely left the hotel. The door was gone. He looked ahead of him and saw space. The background of everything in front of him was a crimson red. There was an odd looking formation of stars that resembled a giant **B**. And right under that formation of stars, was the weirdest thing that Joe had ever seen before. It looked as though the very fabric of time and space had been burned. There was a strong, rotting, burning smell issuing from this area. The giant crack was leaking what look like bits of space to the bottom of nothing.

"You weren't kidding when you said I burned it down were you?" Joe asked.

"No. I wasn't." Aronus said, smoothing up his giant eyelash. Which had grown out two feet since the previous night. "

I'm sorry. I didn't mean to." Joe said.

"I know you didn't kid. But come on. We'll talk back at the hotel." Aronus said.

"How?" Joe asked him as the shadows engulfed him once more.

Chapter 8: Nightmares From The Past

The two of them emerged from the shadows and the door slammed shut behind them. They ventured back down into the lobby and stood there, saying nothing. Finally Joe spoke up.

"How do we get it back?"

"What?" Aronus asked.

"The barrier. How do we get it back?" Joe said.

"Oh don't be ridiculous! Rebuilding the wall would take power that I don't have." Aronus said.

"Then we'll get it back. I'm sure it can't be that-" Joe stopped dead, looking dizzy. Then he looked afraid as a third eye opened up on his forehead. The eye shot a blue beam into midair and a screen appeared. On the screen there was an army. But not a human army. They looked like demons. They were running toward the screen, and they looked angry. The screen disappeared, and the eye vanished.

"What the heck was that?" Joe asked.

"Heather's army. And it would appear that they are indeed going to break free." Aronus said, looking sorrowful.

"No. I meant what just happened to me?" Joe said.

"Oh. That was just your first vision. There are probably gonna be a lot more to come."

"I don't want to have visions. Especially if there's going to be an extra eye opening up on my forehead!" Joe said. "That was just your

45

inner eye. Everyone's got it. It just doesn't normally come out. That's odd."

"Please tell me, that that thing won't appear while I'm in the middle of class." Joe said.

"Oh of course it will. The other people just won't be able to see it." Aronus said. Joe looked horrified at the thought of a large eye appearing on his forehead in the middle of math class.

"Do you know exactly when these visions are?" Joe asked. "Well this one was quite obviously in the future." Aronus replied.

"I could see that. How far in the future?"

"Hard to say. Something like that could be anywhere between a week to a month to a year." Aronus said, screwing up his face as though he were truly confused. "Well I need to know. I need to know how long I have to prepare." Joe said.

"You really think you can fight this?" Aronus asked him.

"I have to try don't I? I mean those things, they looked like they were getting ready to destroy the world. Anyway, I need to go home and get some sleep. I'll be back tomorrow." Joe said. Aronus nodded his head and Joe set off for the dungeons and home.

* * * * *

A young boy of at least eight years old walked into a bedroom. The boy was dressed in a long thick black robe, and it looked as though he had just climbed out of the bed. In this room there was an older girl about 18, with her back to the boy. She looked like she was rummaging through something. Sunlight billowed through the windows like it would never end. The girl's shadow covered the boy's tiny body.

"What are you doing?" The young boy asked her in a high squeaky voice. She turned around, her arms full of coins and dollar bills. The boy looked confused for a moment but then it dawned on him what was happening.

"Why are you stealing our money?" The boy asked her.

"I'm not stealing it. I'm borrowing it. I need it to buy some new clothes." The girl said to him.

"If you don't put that back, I'm telling!" The boy told her.

"No! No you can't tell." She said.

"Yes huh I can! I will unless you put that money back!" He shouted.

"Who do you think you are kid? I'm the baby-sitter. remember? And you will not speak to me in that manner." She said to him.

"Yes huh I will. If you don't put that money back I'm telling my mommy! And she's right up the hall at this time of day." He told her with a triumphant look on her face. "You're not going to say anything to your mother. Now shut the hell up." She said. The boy gasped. And then opened his mouth wide and cried, "Mooooooooooooooooooooooo ooooooooooommmmmmmmmmmmmmmmmmmmmmmmmmyyyyy yyyyyyyyyyyyyyyyyyyyyyyyyyy!" The cry sounded un-earthly to the young girl. His shouts filled the room and every time he stopped, he would take a deep breath and then start again. The girl searched for something to shut the boy up. She searched frantically, until her eyes fell upon the metal handle of the broom that she had been sweeping with earlier. She picked up the broom, rushed over to the screeching boy, raised it high above her head, and hit him over the head with it. He didn't stop screaming so she hit him again, harder this time. The boy stopped abruptly and fell to the floor, a little blood trickling from underneath his bushy black hair. Despite the boy's injury he opened his mouth and began shrieking again. So this time she dragged him from the room and into the kitchen.

Once in the kitchen she searched for something heavier to shut him up. That's when she saw it. The shiny new glass blender that the family had just gotten a few days earlier. She picked up the blender and began beating the boy in the head with it. After a few good hits, and the shattering of the blender, the boy fell silent. The girl went back to the room, grabbed the money and then ran from the front door of the apartment.

The boy spent the next couple weeks in a coma at the local hospital. When he awoke the first thing that his parents did was hold him. Then, once he was released, they dragged him off to court to testify against the baby-sitter. "Do you have anything else to say?" The judge asked the girl. She shook her head.

"Then in the case of Joseph Austin vs. Heather Fellan. The jury finds Heather guilty as charged and she is hereby sentenced to spend the next 67 years in prison for attempted murder of a minor." Heather shot a dirty look at the boy. Then gave him the finger. Ten years later and 670 miles away, the now 18-year-old Joseph Austin woke from his sleep screaming. He looked around his room, sweat pouring down his face. He looked over into the corner and saw a shadow moving.

"Who's there?" He called out into the darkness. No reply came. "Hello?" He called out again. Still no answer. Then suddenly, Heather jumped out at him from the shadows, wielding a large machete.

Chapter 9: The End Of The Worlds

Joe shot up from his bed breathing rapidly. Tears of fright fell from his eyes to join the already down-pouring sweat. He looked around the room, just to be sure that there was nothing lurking in the shadows. He got out of his bed and went over to the window. What he saw made his insides lurch and he wanted to hurl.

Down on the street the were hundreds of Diviantoids. They were gliding around the street, knocking on people's doors and sucking the happiness right out of them. Joe watched them glide around the street below before he heard a knock at his own door. He wrenched his window open and looked down at the door. Sure enough, there was a Diviantoid standing there. The creature knocked again. It kept on knocking. The pounding became louder and louder and stronger and stronger until finally the door broke down.

Joe went under his pillow, seized the golden coin and said the incantation, and the portal opened. Joe jumped through it and no sooner had it closed than a Diviantoid came gliding into his room.

As usual, Joe landed in the middle of the lobby. He looked around and saw Aronus behind the counter. Again, it appeared, filing his obscenely large eyelash.

"Hey Joe. What's up?" He asked him.

"What's up? What's up?! How 'bout this? Diviantoids. Hundreds of them. Gliding around my street and eating people's happiness." Joe said.

"You're kidding right?" Aronus asked, putting the nail file down on the desk.

"Oh yeah. I just came in and made up a story like that." Joe said, furious that Aronus would ask him such a stupid question.

"Well how did they get there?" Aronus asked him.

"How the hell should I know?" Joe replied.

"This is bad. Very, *very* bad." Aronus said.

"Look. All I know is that they were all over my street. When they knocked on a door and the person opened it. They ate them so to speak. One knocked on my door, but no one opened. So they he knocked it down. When I jumped in the portal, I saw a shadow coming towards my door. All those people…" Joe trailed off.

"We'll figure it out. We'll find out why they were there, how they got there, the whole shebang." Aronus said.

Aronus and Joe spent the next few weeks studying in the library of the hotel. They went through books on everything from spells to stop armies of demons to spells to stop armies of mice. After a particularly long night of studying, Joe felt very pleased with himself.

"I think I'm ready." He said to Aronus, shutting a book on positive thinking demons.

"No you're not."

"Why not?!" Joe said.

"You're only one person. This is an army of demons." Aronus said to him.

"So what?" Joe asked him.

"You're not ready. Plain and simple." Aronus said to him.

Defeated, Joe returned the book to the shelf and went upstairs to his bedroom. He opened the door to the hall and ventured down until he reached room 6,845,789. He gave the doorknob a tap with his finger and it opened up. He went inside and flopped facedown on his extremely comfortable waterbed. He let Aronus' words roll around in his head. He was only one person up against an army of demons. He grabbed a pen and paper from his bedside drawer and sat straight up. He put his pen to the paper and let his fingers do the rest.

When he was done, he had (What was in his opinion) a beautifully written spell. He looked it over.

> From the depths of time and space I call, spirits of demon fighters one and all. Assist me in this time of danger, and keep me from looking like a power ranger. Forget assist just battle for me, destroy this army then return to your restings with pinpoint accuracy.

Well it wasn't the most amazing spell ever written, but it was the best that Joe could think of at the moment. He put his first spell in the drawer and laid his head back on the pillow. Thoughts of his own world flooding his mind. *What happened to the rest of the world? Whatever happened, is it my fault?* He decided to check it out. Joe grabbed his coin and said the incantation to get home. He landed safely in his room. Or at least what used to be his room. Everything was different. What was once a lively, bright street, was now a deserted darkened wasteland. Everything was gone. All that was left was rubble. It was though a giant tornado had come ripping through the area, and had left nothing in its wake.

Joe re-opened the portal and stepped through. He wondered if the rest of the world was like this also. He ran up to the library and found the

Aronus had already gone to bed. He wasn't exactly sure where to look for the kind of information that he wanted so he went to several different sections. Once his search was over, he was exhausted. He moved to pick up the books and return them to their proper sections, when he saw that he had forgotten one. The book had an odd title. **Prophecies For Complete And Total Idiots.** Joe wondered to himself why he would pick up a book on prophecies, but opened it anyway.

Mostly there were omens inside. And one particular omen caught Joe's eye. It was an odd sort of *Ja*. It was the exact way that Joe wrote his signature. The book said that when the person bearing these letters as initials entered a certain dimension, it would begin the destruction of the worlds.

"Is it me?" Joe thought aloud. "Am I really the person responsible for all of this?" Joe looked sick. He ran from the library and to the door marked:

The Shadow Zone.

He concentrated on a screen. A screen that would show him all worlds at once. Once he had a clear image of what he wanted, he seized the doorknob and wrenched the door open.

As usual the shadows engulfed him, but he stayed focused on what he wanted. When the shadows cleared, the screen was there. And just as he had feared, there was nothing. Everything was gone. Except for a world directly in front of him. He walked to the left, and then to the right surveying the destruction. Just as he returned to his starting point, the final world was gone. Just like that, it exploded, right before Joe's eyes. He ran from the room, tears forming in his eyes.

Chapter 10: The Village

"Open the damn door!" Joe screamed, pounding on Aronus' door.

"Keep your shirt on!" Joe heard Aronus yell from the other side. He opened the door dressed in an obscenely tight yellow nightgown with an equally tight puke green cap.

"What do you want Joe?" Aronus asked him.

"Why didn't you tell me?" Joe asked through gritted teeth.

"Tell you what?" Aronus asked.

"Tell me that coming here would destroy everything?!?!"

"What are you going on about Joe?" Aronus asked, rubbing the crust out of his eyebrow.

"Everything is gone! All of it!" Joe yelled.

"All of what? What are you talking about?" Aronus asked him.

"All of the worlds. Every last one of them! Obliterated!"

"And how do you figure this is because of you?"

"There's a prophecy book in the library. I checked it there. I didn't want to believe it at first but then I checked for myself. Everything's gone." Joe said.

"Don't worry Joe. We'll get them back." Aronus said to him.

"Oh yeah? How?" Aronus didn't answer. "**HOW?!**" Joe started yelling again.

"Look I don't know. Ok? I don't know how but we will get them back." Aronus said.

"All those people... all of those families. Gone." Joe said, tears once again forming in his eyes. "If everything else was destroyed... why wasn't this place? Why weren't we destroyed with everything else?" Joe asked.

"Apparently, someone or something wants you alive." A thought popped into Joe's head.

"That bitch." Joe said. His teeth gritted.

"Excuse me?!" Aronus said, offended. "We do not use that kind of language in this building. Who are you talking about anyway?" He asked.

"Heather. She has to be behind this. There's no other explanation. She didn't do this alone though. She had to have had help from someone who understood the worlds. Someone who was familiar with all of it. But who?"

Joe pondered this for several hours, and well into the next morning. He couldn't figure out for the life of him who would willingly take part in something so horrible. His thought's lingered for a moment on Principal Hanah, but then realized that even she wasn't this evil. He thought of everyone from Heather's parents to his own parent's ex's. A solid answer never came. Once he had a headache the size of Africa from thinking so hard, he decided to go explore something.

Joe entered the lobby to find it completely empty. Joe thought that it was weird that no one was there. The absence of Aronus frightened him a little bit, but he didn't really think anything of it. He then thought of something, he had never been outside the hotel before. It couldn't be as bad as the rest of the worlds. So he strolled up to the doors, and tried to push them open. While he was pushing, he thought of how much he wanted to get outside. Instead if the doors opening up for Joe, he just fell through.

This was like no place Joe had ever seen before. The grass was greener than he had ever seen. The grass was greener than he had ever seen in his life. And just beyond the field of grass, Joe saw what looked very much like a village. It was unmistakable. Joe walked through the field of grass and flowers. They smelled so wonderful. It was weird, but he felt as though they smelled just like bacon and waffles. Rather than stopping to feast on the flowers, he kept walking. When he reached the edge of the field, and tried to cross between it and the village, he hit a large invisible wall. He stepped back as a large red and gold door materialized. Before he had a chance to push it, it opened. Even though he found this very odd, he went inside.

The first weird thing was that this village was completely empty. There were only shops here. Joe didn't see any buildings that even remotely looked like houses. As he went to explore, he saw that all of the shops were empty. There were no signs in the windows, the signs on the doors said that they were open, but all of the doors were locked. Except one -the door to a shop called "Weapons for everyone". Est. 0001 B.C. was still unlocked, so Joe opened it and went inside. Joe turned on the lights and looked around this shop. There was dust everywhere, but there were also some really cool looking weapons. There was a large sack on the wall, so Joe took it. He started loading up on weapons, but he had no clue why. Then he came to a really cool looking one. It was some type of sword. The handle was a brilliant shade of blue, while the blade was golden. There were two silver snakes curled around the blade. There was a large sign above this sword that said, DO NOT TOUCH!!

But Joe couldn't resist. He took the sword down off of the wall and stuffed it in the bag. Almost instantly, and alarm went off. It sounded shrilly throughout the entire village. Things began to rise out of the ground and step out of the shadows, at least 6 feet tall with completely black eyes. They were draped in black robes and carried large spears.

"Mooshes lui teintus", one of the creatures said, but Joe could understand what it said. It had said, "Return the sword" but Joe wasn't doing it.

"No!", he said back to the creature. It stared at him with its black eyes and then spoke.

"Gur fignor fu ya yuniched!" (Then prepare to be punished). Joe turned around to make a run for it but more creatures blocked the door. He grinned like an idiot and pulled the sword from the bag. He pretended to return the sword on the wall, but instead attacked the nearest creature. He stabbed one, then the snakes came to life and attacked the other two. He fought way through all of the creatures and all the way out the door. Just as he stuffed the sword in the bag, he looked up to see more creatures running towards him.

He shook his head and took off up the street towards the hotel. He reached the door that led back to the field, but it wouldn't open. He pounded and pounded and pounded but the door just wouldn't open. He looked back and saw the creatures gaining on him. He pounded harder and started screaming for someone to let him in. He looked back and the creatures were only 60 feet away. He started pushing on the door and imagining the hotel on the other side. The door cracked a little bit and some light spilled out. The light went straight through the creatures and they deteriorated. Joe looked back at the now open door, and saw a very angry looking Aronus standing on the other side.

Chapter 11: The Cave And The Dragon

"**Just what did you think you were doing**?!" Aronus yelled at him. "You should know better than that!" Aronus yelled at Joe the entire way back to the hotel, and then more once they got there.

"Look, I was just getting supplies. I know that you saw the vision. Lots and lots of demons. So we'll need lots and lots of weapons." Joe said.

"Joe, you stole these weapons!" Aronus yelled.

"It's not like anyone was watching them." Joe said.

"Oh no. No one was watching them Joe. That's why you got chased through the village by Shadow warriors."

"By what?"

"Shadow warriors. Very, *very* strong creatures." Aronus said.

"If they're so strong, then why was I able to get past them?" Joe asked.

"Because they were afraid. They didn't expect you to know how to use the sword." Aronus said.

"And what sword exactly is this?" Joe asked.

"The Sword Of Darkness. It's kind of ironic really. Only the person with the purest heart can even touch it. Which leads me to wonder how you were able to. Either way. This can only mean one thing." Aronus said.

"And what is that?" Joe asked sarcastically.

"That you are the one meant to save the world."

"Ok. Whatever. Look I'm going to take a nap. Those things really tired me out."

Joe went upstairs to his room, and sat on the edge of the bed for a moment. He thought of the sword. Aronus was right. How was able to touch it? Did this mean that he was actually getting some compassion? He didn't know. And he didn't want to think about it anymore until he woke up. So Joe laid back on his pillow and closed his eyes. Within minutes, he was drifting off to sleep.

*_____ *_____ *

Joe was in a cavern of some sort. He walked forward but no end was in sight. So he walked on. And on, and on, and on, and on. Joe walked on for what felt like hours. Eventually he reached an opening. This opening looked very familiar to him. It was large and Joe couldn't see the other side. So he walked forward. Joe stopped suddenly when he heard a voice. He listened closer in hopes of hearing exactly what it was saying.

"Master. I cannot do anything. That do-gooder has the entire building magically protected. We cannot get in." The voice said. The voice was barely over a whisper but Joe could still here what was being said. He moved forward and saw a girl crouched in front of a figure in a dark brown robe. The figure's head was covered up so Joe couldn't see its face. Then a voice came from beneath the hood. "You had better find a way in, or else I'll feed you to Duranga". This voice was louder. This person didn't care about being heard but the voice was disguised, just as (Joe assumed) the person was.

"I cannot! I've tried everything!" The first voice said.

"What part do you not understand? *I WANT HIM DEAD!!!*"
The second voice shouted. This voice was deep. Yet it sounded like the cracking of dead leaves.

"Master, I have been trying since he arrived. And I tried years before now." The first voice said.

"Fine then. Since you can't seem to find your way into that building, perhaps you'll be able to find yourself once you're in Duranga's stomach!" The second voice said.

"Please master! Show mercy upon me. That boy is protected by something. I do not know what, but whatever it is, it's powerful." The girl tucked her strawberry blonde hair behind her ear.

"You have *one* week to get inside of that building and kill that boy or else it'll be you being burned to a crispy cinder", the second voice threatened.

"Got it?" the girl said.

"I mean it!" The hooded figure said and then vanished.

"Stupid wench." the girl said, climbing to her feet. Suddenly something came flying out of the ceiling, and lit the ground on fire. When the girl finally got the fire out she stood back and looked at the area scorched. The fire had burned letters into the ground. The message said simply: I heard that! The girl gave a frightened look and walked away and that's when Joe realized he knew that girl. It was Heather. Joe watched as she disappeared through the stone wall.

Joe walked forward into the clearing, anger pulsing through his veins. He was so pissed off that he missed his chance to pay her back. There was a sudden breeze, a breeze that was weird this deep in (Joe guessed) a cave. He looked up and his mouth dropped open at what he saw. There was something large. It looked suspiciously like a very large rain cloud. Joe could see lightening pulsating inside of it. Even though this struck him as odd, Joe walked away, in the direction that Heather went in. He stuck his hand out to feel the wall that Heather had disappeared into. But there was nothing. It was nothing but solid stone. Suddenly Joe heard a loud thump behind him. He turned around apprehensively and instantly wished that he hadn't. Standing directly under the cloud, was the dragon from Joe's vision. Just as big and ugly as ever. The dragon fixed its large, bright red eyes on Joe and opened its mouth wide. A large jet of fire shot from the dragon's mouth. Joe rolled out of the way just as the fire hit the wall, melting it. Joe got to his feet and ran. He ran back in the direction that he came from, back through the tunnel. He could hear the dragon's monstrous feet running behind him. He ran faster and faster, but the dragon seemed to be gaining on him.

He reached the end of the tunnel in half the time that it took him to reach the clearing. He looked at the wall desperately. There was no door, window, hole or anything else. Just a wall. *So how did I get in?*, Joe thought to himself. He could hear the dragon getting closer and closer. Joe banged on the rock, searching for some way out, some secret passageway or something. But the only thing he got was a very hurt wrist. He turned around, prepared to face the worst. The dragon came to a stop in front of him. During this time before certain death, Joe had the time to see the dragon for what it was. It was a positively ugly creature. Its skin was a sickening shade of green, its horns had very sharp points, and one of its teeth was bleeding. The dragon stepped back a bit, and put its nose to the ground. What happened next was so repugnant and disgusting, that Joe started to feel nauseous. The dragon had let out what sounded like a large burp, and released a sea of lava from its nose. The lava illuminated everything in this cavern, including the dragon. In the light of its own lava, the dragon's skin was a deep shade of red. Then, it stood up straight and put it's nose down to Joe. Opened its mouth and let out another jet of fire. Directly onto Joe.

Chapter 12: Joe's Vision

Joe shot straight up in his bed and instantly checked for burns. There were none. Joe couldn't believe it had all been a dream. He searched desperately around for something telling him that some part had been real. But he found nothing. He reached over to get a pen and paper and could hardly move his wrist. He looked down at it, he saw that it was very bruised and swollen. That was his clue. That was how Joe knew that his dream was not a dream. But then, why wasn't he ash? Why was there still skin on his bones? He didn't know. He looked out the window and saw that it was dark outside. He saw the stars gleaming in the sky. And the very large moon that looked like it was made of crystal. The stars behind it made a very beautiful sight. Joe snapped with his good hand and the lights went out. He looked over at the wall and saw the dots refracted from the star's light. Joe looked more closely. It looked as though the dots were forming words. He got up and got a marker. Went over to the wall, and connected the dots.

When Joe was finished, he turned on the lights, ignoring the stabbing feeling in his wrist as he did so. Sure enough, there was a message on the wall. **Beware the spectral form of the dragon. It shall bring upon the end of The Illurian.**

"What is it with this place and cryptic messages?" Joe asked himself as he left his room and headed towards Aronus'. Since the hand that he usually pounded on the door with was disabled, he yelled inside instead.

"Aronus! Open the door!" He yelled.

Joe heard rustling inside the room, and then Aronus appeared at the door look extremely harassed.

"Do you have any idea what time it is?" He asked, sounding like he was on the verge of murder.

"It doesn't matter." Joe said. "You have to see something in my room." Joe said, and yanked Aronus out of his room and up the hall. He shoved Aronus into his room and pointed at the wall. "What is this supposed to mean?" He asked. Aronus looked at the wall.

"I think it means that the maid did an excellent job while you were sleeping. You can't even see the spaghetti you threw at it."

"What?" Joe asked and turned to inspect the wall for his self. The message was gone. He turned off the light and cried out in pain as his wrist throbbed. Even the sparkles from the moon were gone.

"Oh, what happened to you?" Aronus asked as he flipped the light back on. Aronus took Joe's wrist in his hand. "Now, this is going to hurt you more than it will hurt me." He said.

"Huh? What are you talking about?" Joe asked. Joe howled in agony as Aronus gave his wrist an extremely sharp twist. Joe looked down with tears in his eyes, and saw that his wrist was normal again. There was no swelling or anything. He dried his tears and looked at Aronus. "What did you do?" He asked.

"Don't worry about it. All you need to know is that it was payback."

"What?"

"There was a painless way of doing that. But you woke me up. And dragged me down here for nothing." Aronus said.

"But there was a message on the wall. Really." Joe told him.

"Ok then. What did it say?" Aronus asked. Joe thought for a moment. And then spoke.

"It said, 'Beware the spectral form of the dragon. It shall bring upon the end of the Illurian.'"

"Nice. That was actually really fast compared to most people.

"What are you talking about?" Joe asked, confused.

"That story, it didn't take you as long as it does most people to make up something like that." Aronus said.

"I didn't make that up!" Joe said, offended.

"Of course you didn't Joe. It really said that on the wall. Yeah, and I'm the king of the shrimp kingdom."

"I'm serious! It really said that!" Joe said.

"I believe you Joe. *Really.*" Aronus said.

"Oh yeah! I was in this really weird place while I was sleep. I got chased by a dragon and everything." Joe told him.

"Um… Maybe you should go back to sleep Joe. Rest your mind. I'll see if I can get a shrink in the morning."

"I'm not crazy!" Joe shouted, and vases in his and six neighboring rooms shattered.

"Control your temper!" Aronus spat.

"Then stop talking to me like I'm crazy. Because I'm not. Now look, something did happen to me while I was sleep. I went somewhere. A cave or a cavern or something. And I saw Heather. She was talking to someone. She kept saying master. And they kept talking about breaking into somewhere and killing someone. Then they left and I went to where they were standing to explore. When I was about halfway through this opening, I felt a draft. So I looked up and saw this huge rain cloud. I didn't think anything was wrong so I kept exploring. Then I heard a big thump behind me. And when I turn around, it's the dragon from that vision thingy. It chased me back the way that I came and had me cornered. I started banging on the wall looking for a way out and that's how I hurt my wrist. Then it let an river of lava out of its nose. And spit fire at me." Joe finished. Aronus looked at him.

"If the dragon spit fire at you, how come there are no burns?" Aronus asked.

"I don't know." Joe said. "That's one of the things that's so weird. I get the hurt wrist but none of the burns."

"Joe, you were dreaming. Nothing more, nothing less." Aronus said.

"No. This was more than a dream. This was real. Almost like..." Joe stopped and thought about something.

"Almost like what?"

"Astral Projection." Joe said.

"Impossible! You cannot sustain injuries from astral projection." Aronus said.

"I think you can. It's just really rare."

"Joe. Listen to me. You cannot get hurt while astral projecting. Plain and simple. Now please go back to bed. Before I'm the one that needs a shrink." He turned around to leave.

"Wait!" Joe called out.

"What?" Aronus asked him turning around, clearly annoyed.

"I feel weird." Joe said. "I feel like..." Joe trailed off as once again, a third eye opened up on his forehead and shot a blue beam to the area just above where Aronus was standing. On the screen this time it was Heather and the hooded figure from earlier. And they were talking.

"**WHAT HAPPENED!?!**" The hooded figure shouted at her.

"I don't know it was fine when I left." Heather said.

"**THEN WHY NOW, IS THERE A HUGE HOLE IN THE MIDDLE OF MY CAVERN?!?!?!**" The figure shouted again. And suddenly Joe and Aronus found themselves looking at a very, *very* large hole. The hole looked like it had been created by fire and severe heat. The hole looked like a river of lava, meant to burn Joe to ash, had created it.

Chapter 13: Joe's Visitor

The screen vanished and Joe's third eye closed once more. Aronus looked dumbfounded.

"Y-y-y-y-you were telling the truth." Aronus managed to stutter out.

"Duh! You know, you should really learn to listen to me. Especially concerning matters this important." Joe said.

"You said that they were talking about something..."

"Yeah hold on. Let me see if I can pull up the conversation."

"What?"

"Um... *The plot of the plot remains unseen, so put the plotting up on screen.*" A large screen appeared above their heads.

"Nice spell," Aronus said.

"Thanks."

An image appeared on the screen. Joe was on screen listening for something.

He listened closer in hopes of hearing exactly what it was saying.

"Master. I cannot do anything. That do-gooder has the entire building magically protected. We cannot get in." The voice said. The voice was barely over a whisper but Joe could still hear what was being said. He moved forward and saw a girl crouched in front of a figure in a dark brown robe. The figure's head was covered up so Joe couldn't see its face. Then a voice came from beneath the hood. "You had better find a way in, or else I'll feed you to Duranga." This voice was louder. This person didn't care about being heard. But the voice was disguised, just as (Joe assumed) the person was.

"I cannot! I've tried everything!" The first voice said.

"What part do you not understand? *I WANT HIM DEAD!!!*" The second voice shouted. This voice was deep. Yet it sounded like the cracking of dead leaves.

"Master, I have been trying since he arrived. And I tried years before now." The first voice said.

"Fine then. Since you can't seem to find your way into that building, perhaps you'll be able to find yourself once you're in Duranga's stomach!" The second voice said.

"Please master! Show mercy upon me. That boy is protected by something. I do not know what, but whatever it is, it's powerful." The girl tucked her strawberry blonde hair behind her ear.

"You have *one* week to get inside of that building and kill that boy. Or else it'll be you being burned to a crispy cinder." The second voice threatened.

"Got it." The girl said.

"I mean it!" The hooded figure said and then vanished.

"Stupid wench." The girl said, climbing to her feet. Suddenly something came flying out of the ceiling, and lit the ground on fire. When the girl finally got the fire out she stood back and looked at the area scorched. The fire had burned letters into the ground. The message said simply: I heard that! The girl gave a frightened look and walked away. And that's when Joe realized, he knew that girl. It was Heather. Joe watched as she disappeared through the stone wall.

Aronus stood rooted to his spot for a moment. Looking very upset.

"What's wrong?" Joe asked.

"You're being really naïve, you know that?"

"I'm not being naïve." Joe said. "

Yes you are. You've seen this twice and you still have no clue what they're talking about?" Aronus asked.

"No I don't."

"They're talking about this building and you. I had this place magically protected for your safety. People are trying to kill you Joe. Or don't you get that? Those two, they really don't like you. You cannot go gallivanting off during the night." Aronus told him.

"I didn't gallivant. I don't know how I got there. I told you, I think it was astral projection or something."

"Your physical form cannot be hurt while projecting."

"Obviously it can, because I didn't go anywhere. I really didn't…" Joe tried to explain.

"Joe, you don't think you did. But you must have. That's the only logical explanation."

"Since when does everything have to be logical? Everything about my life since I've met you, has defied all logic. Dragons and other worlds and Diviantoids. None of it is in anyway normal. *You* aren't normal. Everything is completely and totally weird here. Including your guests. None of which I've seen yet. If you can believe all the magical shit that you believe. Why can't you believe me?" He asked.

"I want to believe you Joe. But it's theoretically impossible." Aronus said.

"You are so-" Joe was cut off.

There was a rushing of wind and Joe felt a pulling sensation. Suddenly, he was staring at himself.

"What the hell?" Aronus said, his mouth hanging open.

The new Joe spoke in a voice that echoed through the room. He said: You don't believe me? Believe this. He took one of Aronus' sharpest fingernails and slashed his own arm with it. The real Joe let out an earsplitting scream. He looked down at his arm. It was bleeding. Just like the new one's arm. He spoke again.

"You believe me now?" He then disappeared in a blinding flash of yellow light. Joe felt a pushing sensation as his projection re-entered him.

"Un…frikin…believable." Aronus managed to get out.

"I told you." Joe said, grabbing a towel and holding it to his bloody arm. "By the way, I thought you could only astral project while sleeping." Joe said.

"In this dimension, you can astral whenever you want. You just need to have sincere need to accomplish two things at once. And then of course while you sleep. But I've never seen anyone get hurt while projecting. It's astounding." Aronus looked intrigued.

"It's painful!" Joe told him. Pinching the wound harder. "Cut you freaking nails. And get rid of that eyebrow!" Joe said, his arm going numb with pain.

"Oh calm down you big baby. It'll heal." Aronus told him.

"It will not! I'm going to have a scar for the rest of my life."

"Oh you will not." Aronus said, waving his hand. Suddenly the pain was gone from Joe's arm. He removed the towel and the cut, as well as any trace of blood on his arm, was gone.

"How did you do that?" Joe asked.

"I thought you would know by now Joe, I can do anything." Aronus said before leaving.

Joe shut the door behind Aronus and turned off the light. He turned around and Heather jumped out of the shadow next to the window, and plunged a knife deep into his stomach.

Joe felt excruciating pain as he looked down at his bloody stomach. He looked up at Heather.

"Nighty night Joe." Heather said, smirking.

"Fuck you." Joe said. He grabbed Heather's arm and used it to wrench the bloody knife from his stomach. He punched her and she fell to the ground.

"I've been waiting so very long for this", he said and pulled her up from the ground. He carried her over and hurled her out of the window. Glass shattered everywhere as she went through and began her descent.

Joe left his room, clutching his wound as he walked up the hall. He stopped in front of Aronus' door and banged on it .

"WHAT?!?" He screamed from his bed. Joe could hear him moving around inside. He pulled the door open. "Joe... what happened to you?"

"Heather..." Joe rasped out as the last of his energy left his body. He felt to the ground and fought the approach of death. After a moment it was like the shadow zone. He was engulfed by the darkness.

Chapter 14: The Beginning Of The End

Joe is walking through a long hallway. He looks around and sees hundreds of doors. Every step, there's a door. He reaches the end and finds a large oak door. The door has a large golden knob. He twists the knob and pushes the door open. Inside the room there is row upon row upon row upon row of CD cases. all with demonic looking symbols on them. He walks forward and sees another door. This one had a truly demonic looking symbol on it. It appeared to be demon, sacrificing a turkey. The only thing was that they were all connected by different lines. He walked toward the door and spoke.

"Flardet uins y Intelusop."

The door began to glow a violent shade of green. It lifted from the ground about half an inch and hovered for a second. Joe could hear rumbling from inside. The door lifted the rest of the way. Joe was staring at a room filled with demons. But none of them noticed him. They appeared to be digging a hole. Joe stepped into the room and the door lowered to a close behind him. The floor was nothing but dirt, as if he was standing on bare earth. There was a bump in the ground but Joe didn't see it. He tripped and fell directly on his face. He heard a very loud collective growl and all other sounds in the room stopped. Even though his better judgment warned him against it, Joe lifted his head.

He was staring a horde of demons in the face. The nearest one had bright green skin, eyes all over its face, and grotesque bodily features.

As Joe jumped to his feet, the demons started advancing on him. He backed up until he couldn't back up anymore. When the demons got too close, Joe made a run for it. He ran up the wall (something he never knew he could do) and around the demons. A little way past them, he fell. He got up and continued running, the demons gaining on him. He tripped on the edge and tumbled into the hole that the demons were digging. He hit the ground and saw demons jumping down in the hole after him. The closest demon (which oddly resembled a TV star with horns), pulled a sword from its belt and drove it in the direction of Joe's gut.

Joe awoke screaming and clutching his gut. He startled Aronus out of a sound sleep.

"What's on earth is wrong with you?" Aronus asked, looking a bit angry that Joe had once again woken him from a sound sleep at an obscene hour. Joe looked down at his gut. There was not any blood, but there was a large gauze wrapping up his stomach. Slowly, his encounter with Heather came back to him.

"How long was I out?", he asked.

"A week."

"What?!? It only felt like a couple of hours."

"Well it was a week. Now what on earth were you yelling about?" Aronus asked, beginning to get impatient.

"I think I astraled again. It may have been a dream, but it felt way too real."

"Where'd you go?" Aronus asked, half intrigued.

"I don't know. It was some kind of room. A hall at first. Then a room. All leading to this really weird looking door."

"What did this room look like?"

"A bunch of rows. With shelves with all these demonic looking CD cases I guess. And the door had this really odd symbol on it. And I said something and it just opened. The room had the army of demons that I saw and they were digging a hole. I was walking towards them but I tripped and they heard me, and charged. I did some running around before falling into the hole and them jumping in after me. Just when one was ready to stab me in the gut, I woke up." Joe finished. Aronus sat rooted to his spot. His mouth frozen open in a dazed kind of look. "Uh… You okay?" He asked.

"Not really. Aronus continued. Have you ever been in the basement?" Joe nodded. "Not the dungeons, The Basement." Joe shook his head. "Then that can't have been a dream, because everything you just described to me up to the door is in the basement. And you said the door opened for you after you said something?" Joe nodded. "What did you say?"

"I don't know. It was a different language. I didn't even understand it. So what you're saying… is that all of that is in the basement?"

"Yeah. But I never knew about the demons. They must have been there for a while."

"So what do we do?" Joe asked.

"We fight."

"Are you crazy? There are millions of those things in there. I'm not fighting them." He thought about it for a moment. "Nope. Not fighting."

"Fine. Then they'll get out and overrun the dimension.

"No they won't."

"How do you know?"

"I know. That's all you need to worry about. So… when can I get out of here?"

"The doctors said as soon as you wake up."

"Then I'm leaving. Bye bye." And with that he hopped out of bed and left through the double doors.

He wasn't sure how he knew the way back to his room. But he knew it. He reached his room and sat on his bed. He was afraid to go to sleep, but he was afraid to stay awake too. If he slept, he'd astral. If he stayed awake, he'd plot. He didn't want to do either. Suddenly, his third eye opened up and shot its beam towards the door. As usual, the screen appeared, and on the screen, an image. This one was weird though. It showed the door from earlier. And the hooded figure from the cavern in front of it.

"Flardet uins y Intelusop!" The voice cried. The door lifted from the ground and hovered for a moment, then raised the rest of the way. The figure cleared its throat. The demons all turned around. "It's time to go." It said and disappeared. Then the screen switched to the lobby, and a large portal that had opened in front of the door. The screen vanished and Joe's eye closed.

"Oh no." Joe said and jumped off his bed and ran from the room once more. Downstairs, there was the portal right in front of the door. And there were the demons running through it to freedom. The last one looked at him and winked. And the portal closed. Joe stood there dazed, as the demons went on to ravish the remains of the worlds.

Chapter 15: Back In Time

Joe raced back up the stairs and back into his hospital room. He was relieved to find Aronus still sitting in his chair. He looked like he was getting back into a nice sleep. Joe shook him awake. Aronus opened his eyes and looked at Joe.

"If you wake me up in the middle of the night one more time, I'm throwing you out." He said in an annoyed voice.

"You wouldn't do that." Joe said, breathing hard.

"And why not?"

"Because there's an army of demons waiting to ravage anyone who steps foot in any of the worlds."

"What are you talking about?"

"The hooded person, from my little astral session, she was here. She was in the basement, and released the demons. Then she opened a portal for them to get out of hotel and left." Joe explained.

"And how exactly do you know this Joseph?" Aronus asked, annoyed.

"I had a vision. And I saw it. When I got downstairs, the last demons were going through the portal. Then I came up to see you."

"But there's nothing left of the worlds to ravage." Aronus said.

"There will be." Joe said.

"What are you talking about?"

"I have a plan. But first: I've been reading and re-reading that prophecy. That book is brand new. That prophecy was only just written. By Heather's boss. And Heather is the one that destroyed everything. So I kill her, everything comes back." Joe told him.

"That doesn't make sense Joe. First, if she's powerful enough to do all of that, you are nowhere near powerful enough to stop her. Second, if you do kill her, you can't exactly steal her powers and use them for yourself."

"I know that. That's why I'm not fighting her now. I'm fighting her 10 years ago today."

"July 13th 1994? Why that date?" Aronus asked.

"Because, that's the day she did this to me." Joe said and reached for his neck.

He grasped something and lifted. He had pulled off a mask. Underneath was the exact same face, but it was badly mangled. There were stitches stitching up places that never should have been torn. His face was badly bruised and half of his nose was gone. Aronus looked on in horror as Joe pulled the mask back on.

"Joe… why didn't you show me before?" Aronus asked.

"I haven't showed anyone. I didn't want anyone to know. And no I won't show you exactly what she did." Joe said.

"Ok… then at least answer me this question: How do you plan on going back to stop her? You don't have any kind of time traveling powers."

"I'll get some." Joe said. "I'm going to stop her though." Joe said.

"Ok, then once the worlds are back, what are you going to do about the demons?"

"I'm going to bring them back here before I kill her. I need to go. See you later." Joe left the room.

He walked back to his own room and once again, plopped down on the bed. He took his pen and paper from the drawer and turned to a fresh page. He put the pen to paper and started to write.

> Open the portal hear my rhyme, take me back through space and time. To the 13th of July 1994, take me back without the roar.

He was satisfied with this one so he started the next.

> Open the portal hear my rhyme, take me forward through space and time. To the 13th of July 2004, take me forward without the roar.

He had a spell to get there and back, now he needed one for the demons.

> Powers of the Austin's rise, we're unseen across the skies. The demons come forth are the scourge of hell, so take them back to the Illurian hotel.

He now had all the spells that he needed. Now all he needed was to prepare.

Joe went under the bed and got his sword. He thought of something.

"*Shrink!*" he hissed and the sword shrunk in his hand. He stuffed the sword in his pocket and got his four spells. He grabbed a bottle of water from the fridge and put it in his other pocket. He made up his mind, he was finishing this tonight. He was killing her off once and for all. He turned to the time travel spell and opened his mouth.

"Open the portal hear my rhyme, take me back through space and time. To the 13th of July 1994, take me back without the roar."

What happened next was in direct violation of the spell. Joe heard a loud *toooooooooooooooooooooooooooooooooooooooooottttttttttttt*. And when he looked out his window there was a train there. A short bald man pulled open the door right in front of Joe's face.

"Time Travel Express. Train Destination, 1994." He spoke with a loud voice. He then looked down at Joe and yanked him onboard the train.

This train was the oddest that Joe had ever seen before. There was writing on the window and dirt on the floor. In addition, the floor was moving. Joe went and took his seat as the train sped off through time. He heard screaming in the next car, and saw a woman running through. She was closely followed by a man in a green hockey mask. He threw a spear at her and it caught through the head, pinning her to the door. He walked up and yanked her and the spear from the door. He looked at Joe and gave him a look that said "She's mine!" He then sunk directly into the ground.

That happened several more times. Joe later discovered that the things in the hockey masks were called Time Eaters. They would go through the cars on the train and eat people who weren't supposed to be there. One tried to take Joe. So he showed it the spell and it didn't care and still wanted to eat him. So he took it's spear and drove it through its eye.

After another half an hour, the train slowed and stopped. Joe looked and saw his parent's old bedroom and knew that they had gone to the right place. But when the doors opened, instead of him getting off in the room, the car was filled with a bright light from somewhere. Figuring he had nothing to lose, Joe stepped into the blinding white light.

Chapter 16: Heather

A young boy of at least eight years old walked into a bedroom. The boy was dressed in a long thick black robe, and it looked as though he had just climbed out of the bed. In this room there was an older girl about 18, with her back to the boy. She looked like she was rummaging through something. Sunlight billowed through the windows like it would never end. The girl's shadow covered the boy's tiny body.

"What are you doing?" the young boy asked her in a high squeaky voice. She turned around, her arms full of coins and dollar bills. The boy looked confused for a moment but then it dawned on him what was happening.

"Why are you stealing our money?" the boy asked her. "I'm not stealing it. I'm borrowing it. I need it to buy some new clothes," the girl said to him.

"If you don't put that back, I'm telling!" the boy told her. "No! No you can't tell," she said.

"Yes I can! I will unless you put that money back!" he shouted.

"Who do you think you are kid? I'm the baby-sitter remember? And you will not speak to me in that manner," she said to him.

"Yes huh I will. If you don't put that money back I'm telling my mommy! And she's right up the hall at this time of day," he told her with a triumphant look on her face. "You're not going to say anything to your mother. Now shut the hell up," she said. The boy gasped. And then opened his mouth wide and cried, "Mooooooooooooooooooooooooooo ooooommmmmmmmmmmmmmmmmmmmmmmmmmyyyyyyyyyyyy yyyyyyyyyyyyyyyyyyyyy!" The cry sounded un-earthly to the young girl. His shouts filled the room and every time he stopped, he would take a deep breath and then start again. The girl searched for something to shut the boy up. She searched frantically, until her eyes fell upon the metal handle of the broom that she had been sweeping with earlier. She picked up the broom, rushed over to the screeching boy, and raised it high above her head. A hand grabbed her and she looked over and saw Big Joe looking at her with a look of pure hate in his eyes.

"Who the hell are you," she asked, fear visible in her eyes.

He looked at her, and said: "I'm Big Joe." And with that he flung her across the room. He looked down at his younger self, who had now stopped screaming.

"You ok?" he asked.

"Yeah," Young Joe said.

"Ok. Go up the hall and get your mom. Stay up there with her and don't come back until she does. But don't tell her I'm here ok?" The young Joe nods. "Now go." The boy gets up and runs from the room.

Joe grabbed the broom from the ground and goes over to her. He looked at the broom handle like it was life. And in a way it was. It was the key to the end of a nightmare that lasted ten long years. His entire life in the future depended on his actions at that very moment. He then looked at Heather and she looked terrified.

"Why do you look so afraid? You were about to kill me."

"Please... Please don't kill me." Heather pleaded.

"Burn in hell!" Joe said and started beating her viciously with the broom handle. All of the anger that had been building up inside of him for the last ten years was released. All of the pain, all of the fear, all of every bad feeling that he had felt in the last ten years came out in each vicious blow. He stopped and stepped back to see what he had done.

Heather was bleeding badly from every socket on her face. Her left eye hung disgustingly from the socket and her right eye didn't exist anymore. It was floating around somewhere inside her preparing to be dissolved. Her breath was ragged and shallow.

"Please... Please... I don't wanna die," She managed to gasp out.

"Well... neither do I." He took his note pad out of his pocket and turned to the last spell that he wrote. "Powers of the Austin's rise, we're unseen across the skies. The demons come forth are the scourge of hell, so take them back to the Illurian hotel." He then pulled the mini sword from his pocket. *"Enlarge!"* He hissed and the sword grew back to normal size. He raised the sword high above his head and drove it directly into Heather's heart. The two snakes came to life and uncoiled their bodies from the blade of the sword and went straight for her neck. With one clean bite from each, her head was completely taken off.

He stepped back and re-shrunk the sword, then stuffed it back into his pocket. He summoned the train home and boarded. The Time Eaters could smell the stench of death on him, so they didn't mess with him. He arrived back at the hotel in no time. When he got off the train memories flooded him that he never experienced before. Memories of life after Heather's death. He rushed over to the mirror and tried to pull off the mask. But he couldn't. It wasn't a mask anymore. He had his regular face back. Being that it was morning now, he rushed down to the lobby and saw Aronus.

"Hey Aron-" But then remembered, Aronus wouldn't remember him. With all the changes he had made in history, he realized that he shouldn't have come back to the hotel. No one would know him.

"Don't worry," Aronus said to him. "I cast a spell to shield me from your changes. I remember you. By the way, your demon shipment came in. They're all in the basement."

"Then let's go." Joe said and headed off to the basement, reaching for the final spell. Aronus was following close behind him.

"I thought you weren't going to fight them." Aronus said.

"I'm not." Joe said, ignoring the confused look on Aronus' face. He opened the door to the basement and looked down.

"HEY!" Joe yelled. All of them looked up. "From the depths of time and space I call, spirits of demon fighters one and all. Assist me in this time of danger, and keep me from looking like a power ranger. Forget assist just battle for me, destroy this army then return to your resting with pinpoint accuracy!" There was a deep rumbling and a large milky looking dragon appeared next to Joe. It flew down into the basement and light instantly flooded it all. The demons were all flooded in light and were overtaken. There was screaming and yelling as they were destroyed.

The ground beneath them beneath them began to quake violently.

"Let's go!" Joe shouted and they both took off. When they were back in the lobby Aronus looked back and saw the ground caving in.

"Oh damn it!" he said and kept running. They ran out the door and onto the lawn and out a little then turned around. They watched the Illurian hotel cave into the ground.

"You idiot!" A voice said from behind them before Aronus had the chance to. They both turned around and saw the hooded figure. Heather's master.

"She's dead!" Joe said, looking triumphant.

"I know." The figure said, finally dropping its robe. Joe instantly recognized makeup and wrinkles.

Chapter 17: Heather's Boss

"You." Joe said.

"Good morning Joseph." She said. Joe was staring Principle Hanah in the face.

"Why?" Joe asked. Puzzled as to why his principle would try to kill him.

"It's simple Joseph, you're a danger to me. Look at what you did to my beautiful hotel."

"Excuse you missy, this is my hotel!" Aronus said, obviously offended.

"It would have been mine, if that blonde bimbo had killed you two like I told her to. Now prepare to face the most powerful witch in the world!", she bellowed.

"Wait a sec, why did you try to kill me ten years ago?" Joe asked.

"Because, I saw this union, and your attempts to stop me."

"Oh ok. You said the most powerful witch?" She nodded. "Most powerful *evil* witch?" She nodded. "Ok." He pulled his water from earlier from his pocket and threw it on her. She let out shrill blood curdling scream. She took her hands away from her face and Joe felt like puking. Her face had become a grotesque skeleton face. And the last of her head slowly burned away. Until it was nothing but a skull.

"You are going to pay for my face! You little turd!" It was really weird watching her talk. But it was really funny too. Just words where the lips where supposed to be flapping and sound coming out. Joe and Aronus started laughing. "Don't you dare laugh at me you insolent little warts. AAAAAAAAAAHHHHHHHHHHHH!" She screamed and shot a lightning bolt from her hand. Both of them jumped out of the way and the bolt hit the only remaining wall from the hotel. Aronus whimpered as the last remaining piece of the Illurian hotel crumbled into the large crater. Joe was running and dodging lightning when he tripped. He looked at the item that had tripped him up. It was a mirror. Another lightning bolt shot at him and he grabbed the mirror and sent the bolt back in the direction that it came in. It hit Principle Hanah and she began to shake violently, electricity reverberating through her body. The skin exploded from her body and nothing was left but the bones. Joe thought it odd that the bones were connected but he didn't say anything. He went over to stare into the crater of what was left of the Illurian hotel. He looked down into the wreckage and saw something weird. There was no debris down there. It was magma. Joe could feel the heat even on the back of his neck. He turned around and saw a beam of fire coming at him. He saw the dragon, and the skeleton riding it. Aronus was running around at the bottom of the hill, hoping someone would open the door. Meanwhile Joe was up here by himself, preparing for a fight against a dragon.

The dragon shoots another beam of fire at him and he dodges it. The dragon chases after him with Principle Hanah shouting orders from its back. Beams of fire are constantly being shot at him, but he continues dodging them. He racks his mind looking for something that can protect him.

"Invisible walls on one another build, protect me with layers of a shield", Joe said not sure if it would work. The dragon shot another beam at him but this time it stopped several inches from Joe's face. The shield was only temporary was so Joe had to work quickly.

"Up in the air with no where to land, give me leftover fire power in the palm of my hand!" Instantly, a fireball appears in his hand. He throws it at the dragon and it shrieks in agony.

But the ball barely makes a scratch.

"Dammit", Joe exclaimed. The dragon shot another beam of fire and another ball appeared in Joe's hand. He thought for a second and then hurled it at the dragon's head. It hits it right between the eyes. Joe could see fire between the dragon's eyes. Within minutes, the fire had engulfed the dragon's body and Principal Hanah's skeleton. Within another few minutes, both skeletons were on the ground, badly burned. In order to avoid another resurrection, Joe used all the strength he had to lift every last bone and drop it into the crater. Twenty minutes later, Joe had the last bone. Principal Hanah's skull.

"Burn in hell", he said as he tossed it into the crater and walked away. He heard a loud rumbling and turned around, his eyes wide in fear. The ground around the crater was shaking violently.

Suddenly, Joe saw lava erupting from the ground. He took off running down the hill with the lava close behind him. He reached the door to outside to find Aronus still banging. He looked back and saw that the lava was less than thirty yards away. He started banging with Aronus, yelling for someone to open up. The door opened and both ran threw. The lava was ten feet away from the door. He thought desperately about closing the door and it slammed shut just as the lava reached it. He looked on the other side of the door by way of the invisible barrier. There was nothing left. All that was there was a smoking hole. And only one thought crossed Joe's mind. It was finally over.

Chapter 18: Prophecy Boy

Joe landed safely in what was once again his bedroom. He looked out his window. There were no Diviantoids roaming the streets. The streets were streets again, not desert wastelands. Everything appeared to be as it should have been. There was just one thing left to check out. Joe went downstairs, expecting to see his parents in the kitchen sipping coffee. But when he got there, there was no one. Even the puddles of blood were still on the floor. Which could only mean one thing. Heather didn't take his parents. He opened the portal and returned to the ruins of the hotel.. He opened the door and stared out at the two-mile wide crater.

And then he remembered. The glass. He had never gotten on the other side. Aronus said that his parents were over there. It was weird. Only two hours ago, there had been a grand and majestic building standing over this monstrous crater. Now it was nothing. And it was all Joe's fault. Suddenly, he remembered the warning on his room wall. "Beware the spectral for of the dragon. It shall bring upon the end of the Illurian." It was right. The souls of all the demon fighters in history banded together and formed on big dragon. It destroyed all the demons sure. But it also destroyed the hotel. There was nothing he could do about it now. So why worry?

Just as Joe turned to walk away he saw a light, coming out of the crater. He turned back around and saw light stretching across the entire crater. Even though (again) his better sense warned him against it. Joe put his foot on the light. It was sturdy. So he put the other on it. And was instantly pulled along the rest of it. He was pulled at a very high speed and at one point the light started to incline. Joe suspected this was where the steps once where. There was a very sharp incline and Joe nearly fell off. And about five flights up it straightened out. This was the roof. Then it inclined, but it wasn't that steep. This was the same light that Joe rode his first visit to the hotel. After a while he could see the glass. Just as last time, when he got close, a hole opened up. He speeded towards the glass, expecting to fall off again. But he didn't. He went straight through the hole and fell right on his face on the other side.

Joe looked up and saw a vast forest.

"Oh come on!" Joe said, annoyed. He walked forward towards the forest. When he got to the entrance of the forest, two of the trees jumped in his path.

"You have got to be kidding me", Joe said.

"Present the password or perish", one of the trees said.

"Get out of my way you annoying future packs of paper!", Joe said. "Password accepted." The trees said in unison and jumped out of Joe's way. Confused, Joe walks deeper into the forest.

A mile and a half in, Joe reached a clearing. This clearing is filled with even more demons. More than the first time. Joe thought of backing away and going home, but then he looked across the clearing and saw two people chained to trees. His parents. But how was he supposed to get across there? He couldn't possibly risk his parents and call that dragon again. But then he thought of something. He pulled the sword from his pocket and enlarged it. If this sword was supposed to be all-powerful, then maybe he could channel some power through it.

He closed his eyes and let power run through his body. He raised the sword to the sky and points it at the sky just above the demon's heads.

He opened his mouth wide and bellowed: *"Petrinolious!"* The demons all turned around and looked as though they were getting ready to charge , but they all froze over.

Joe was looking at an army of demons that were now solid ice. It was actually quite astounding, yet humorous. Joe let out a loud primal yell and attacked. He used his sword and the snakes to destroy every last block of ice in the clearing until the was only one thing left. But it had its back to Joe and it wasn't frozen.

"Turn around and fight!", Joe boldly challenged, prepared to fight whatever was under that coat.

"My pleasure", the voice sounded very familiar to Joe. But he couldn't figure out who it was. The figure turned around. Joe thought that he was prepared for everything, but he wasn't prepared for this.

Aronus was staring him in the face. A crooked smile on his face.

"Why?" Joe asked even more confused than when he entered the forest.

"Isn't it obvious Joseph? I needed you to get me the sword."

"Don't call me Joseph", he said through clenched teeth.

"I'll call you whatever I want to. This is my world!" He said, looking quite demented.

"Why couldn't you get someone else to get the sword?", Joe asked.

"Because I needed you."

"But why?"

"Oh come on Joseph. Were you always this stupid? That prophecy? It wasn't fake, it was changed. I had the real book all the time" Aronus threw the book at Joe and it automatically opened up to the right page. Joe picked it up and read it aloud.

"When the person bearing the initials 𝒥𝒜 (JA) enters the dimension which contains the Illurian stone in the two thousand and fourth year, in the seventh month, he shall be able to take the sword of darkness. And whoever duels him, and beats him, shall become the most powerful entity in any of the worlds."

"Do you get it now?"

"But… you… you helped me" Joe said.

"Well you had to trust me didn't you? If you hadn't come, I wouldn't have the chance to take the sword from you." Aronus told him.

"But what about Heather and Hanah?"

"Well I hired Heather to kill you when you were younger. But then I thought about it. Why kill you *before* I got the sword?

Why not kill you with it? She failed anyway, but that's beside the point. And I hired Hanah when I found out how much you hated her. I mean how classic is that? Attacked by the person you hate the most", Aronus continued.

"But the visions…"

"You were never supposed to get them. You weren't supposed to get any powers. But I figured I could make it work to my advantage. I knew you wouldn't be able to control them, making you a danger to yourself."

"But Heather…"

"She was beginning to get stupid. So she needed to die. And who better for the job? I mean Joseph honestly… why do you think that I didn't help you earlier? I was counting on that incompetent redheaded wench to kill you. But she failed, so she deserved to die. Do you understand it now Joseph?" Aronus asked him.

"Do not call me Joseph." He said through gritted teeth.

"Joseph Joseph Joseph Joseph." Aronus taunted. Joe squeezed the handle of the sword. He felt electricity surging through it.

"Do Not Call Me Joseph!" he demanded, squeezing the handle harder.

"What are you going to do about it? Joseph Ashley Austin." This time he had gone too far. Joe let out a yell that came from the very depths of his soul. It was so loud and so powerful that it seemed to shake the trees from the roots up and the entire forest.

Joe charged, still yelling sword raised high in the air. He started to bring the sword down but moved it back and drop kicked Aronus instead. He used every angry emotion that he had ever felt and pretended that Aronus was at the root of them. He didn't hold anything back. With Heather, he had held back because she was a girl. But this was different. Aronus had betrayed him. He had made him trust him and then betrayed him. He had used him. That was inexcusable.

When he stopped, Aronus was bruised and extremely bloody. There was blood and a bruise on every visible patch of skin. Joe figured that he should have let him fight back a little, but he was too angry and hurt to stop. He went over to the tree that his mother was tied to.

"You were a good trainer." He cut the chains that tied her up and walked over to his father's tree. "A friend even." He cut the chains that tied up his father. He walked back over and stood in front of Aronus.

Aronus looked up at him and Joe saw how pitiful he was, that eyelash over the one eye that he could see out of. But he didn't have any compassion.

"For a friend, I'll make it quick." And with that, he shoved the sword through Aronus' skull. The skull shattered on impact and his head kind of melted down on his neck. There was just skin laying on top of a heap of shattered shards of bones.

"Oh Joe." His mother sighed and ran over to hug him. His father did the same thing. When his parents let him go he looked around the field at what he had done. He wondered if his parents had thought that he was a murderer.

"Mom... dad... do you guys think that I'm a killer?"

"Yes you are a killer son." His father said.

"But you killed to save people. And yourself. So it's excusable." His mother said.

"I don't know what came over me. I just... lost it. Everything that I had ever felt, all the pain, all the fear, all the anger. It was released on him." Joe told his parents.

"Come on Joe. We'll talk more at home." His mother said.

"Ok. *Carrez Mahset Littstella.*" Joe said. And the portal back home opened. His parents stepped through first. Joe took one final look at his dead mentor. He felt the sadness overwhelm him. He couldn't block them anymore. The tears came and streamed down his cheeks. He walked through the portal, and left the world of the former Illurian Hotel behind.

"Welcome to the ceremony for the promotion of the graduating class of 2004!" The MC shouted through the crowded school auditorium. Joe had waited thirteen long years for this moment. He was finally getting out of school. In the last month, he had gotten more in touch with the powers presented to him by the historical Illurian hotel. He had even discovered a few new ones. He had learned to control his telekinesis, astral projection, and had even learned to call on his eye to see through walls. As the MC spoke and turned over the mic to several other speakers, Joe thought about everything that brought him here. All the battles and the visions, and even his highly successful spells.

Just as Joe started thinking about how much he missed the hotel, the MC spoke something not as boring.

"And now, introducing the graduating class of 2004! George Amilius!" A short stubby boy went up and gladly accepted his diploma. "Joseph Austin!" Joe rose from his seat and walked across the stage, smiling proudly. He felt a surge of pure joy as he accepted the little rolled up piece of paper certifying his school completion. He walked back to his seat and sat down still smiling. He suddenly felt a pulling sensation and instantly was seeing two different places. On one side was the graduation but on the other he was staring at a girl, tall and apparently starved. Her face was very pale and her stomach clung to her bones making her look like an underfed skeleton. She looked up at him and he could see that she had blonde hair and blue eyes.

"Please... help me!" She spoke in a very high whisper. She reached in her pocket and pulled out a map. She placed it in Joe's hand and he felt an instant sucking sensation. Suddenly he was only seeing single again. But there was one difference. The map was still in his hand. He opened the map up and looked at it. He could tell one thing. That he was going to be in this for a very, *very* long time.

PART 2:
THE BEGINNING

Chapter 1: The High Demons Of The Tower

"AAAAAAAAAAAHHHHHHHHHHHHHHHHHHHH!!!! MOTHER OF GOD!" Aronus cried out after being electrocuted for the 5,627th time. **"Please! Please STOP!"**

"Why should we stop? You have failed us repeatedly. We ask you to do something as simple as kill a teenager. And you couldn't even do that. You put us all to shame! So tell us. If you cannot do what we ask of you. Why should we do what you ask of us?"

"Because it was not as simple as just killing him. This boy was driven by rage. There was no stopping him." Aronus said.

"We have sent someone else in you place. Perhaps *she* will be able to end him. You have disgraced us all. You allowed him to destroy the one thing that keeps everything separate. Without The Illurian Hotel, The worlds will bleed into one another. Everything in all worlds will die horrible deaths unless we find a way to right what you have wronged", One of the High Demons Of The Tower said.

"I can right it", Aronus told them.

"How can you right anything when your body has been destroyed", another asked.

There were five demons in The Order. The Order of the High Demons Of The Tower was an elite secretive order bent on domination of all of the worlds. They wanted to be the kings of the universe.

The demons were, Odesson, the weakest demon in the Order. Yet he was still strong enough to rip apart an entire country in a matter of minutes. Then there was Huidon, he was the logical thinker of the group, but still powerful. Pysuil was the more diabolical one. Kurg was second in command, and Migued was the leader and most powerful.

"I'll find a way. No one kills me and gets away with it." Aronus said through gritted teeth.

"Well he'll just have to this time," Odesson said. "Resume the torture!!" He yelled and once again, electrical bolts coursed through Aronus' body. Aronus cried out in anguish as his skin started to smoke. The smell of his own cooking flesh was not one that he particularly cared for. He looked up at Migued who had a no expression at all on his face. He merely looked on. No interest or intrigued showed. Not even mild amusement.

Tears began to fall from Aronus' eyes. The more he cried, the more electricity shot through his body. Just when he felt like he would explode, the shocking stopped.

"We have discussed it, and we have decided that you shall be allowed one more chance to kill the boy. You will be assisted by Julya. Should you fail this time, we shall resume your torture for the next millennia and we shall take him down ourselves. Do you understand?" Migued asked him. Aronus nodded. "DO YOU UNDERSTAND!?" His voice boomed throughout the room.

"Yes." Aronus said.

"Good," Migued said. "Oh and by the way, you might want to take these. They may come in handy." He took seven blue cubes from his pocket. Each had a number on it. 001, 599, 648, 045, 587, 214 and 666.

He tossed the cubes at Aronus. "In order to activate them, just toss it in the air and say activate." Aronus picked the cubes up from the floor and examined them. "Now get out of my sight!" he said. A hole opened under Aronus' feet and he fell through.

"Do you think that we can trust him," Kurg asked.

"Of course not. But maybe he won't be sent here this time. The boy will kill him again for sure. And then it's our turn. One way or the other, he will die.

Aronus landed face first on a hard stone floor. He swore loudly as he got up and noticed that his nose was bleeding. He looked up and saw the girl who gave Joe the map standing in front of him.

"So nice of you to finally make it," she said in an annoyed voice. "For future reference, if you're not on time, I kill you." She turned around and began walking, after a few feet she stopped and looked back. "What? Do you need a special invitation? Bring your lazy good for nothing ass on here." Aronus followed. She led him for at least a mile and into a cave in the middle of the forest. "Now in case you're too slow to have noticed already, I'm Julya. And I don't take crap from flunkies. Now things can go one of two ways. You can do exactly what I say when I say do it, or I can kill you and send back to where ever you were before you were dumped on me."

She snapped her fingers and her appearance instantly changed. She looked well fed and well dressed. Her hair was tied up into a bun and she had two daggers holding it in place.

"Well it's nice to meet you Julya, I'm-"

"I didn't ask." She said and walked away. Aronus followed her deeper into the cave and found two doors. "Now, don't touch these doors unless I tell you to, understood?" He nodded. "Good. The reason is because these doors both lead into a very dark place also known as the realm of shadows. Now I'm sure you know Joe, correct?" He nodded, a look of disdain in his eye. "Good. I've given him a very detailed map that leads directly into the realm of the shadows."

"What will it do? The realm of shadows I mean."

"It will devour him. With a little help from the two of us, it will destroy every essence of his being."

"I hope you know that it's not easy to kill this boy. He's taken down two very powerful women, a dragon, and me." Aronus told her.

"Well there's a very simple explanation for that. You're all *weak*. I don't understand how you can't take down a simple teenager and steal a sword from him. That is truly the dumbest thing that I've ever heard. You are a disgrace to all warrior kind. You put your mother to shame. She's probably turning over in the ruins of that run-down old shack you called a hotel."

"Now look here. I'll have you know that my hotel was one of the most powerful places in any of the worlds!"

"Yeah right", Julya snickered. "I happen to know that your run-down old shack was just a rip off of the real thing. And the real thing happens to be a thousand times more powerful than your little fantasy house."

"It is not!" Aronus said.

"So you admit that there's another one. A *real* one?"

"Mines in real..." Aronus said. Not really convinced anymore.

"Yeah ok," Julya said. "You just keep on telling yourself that." She began to walk away.

"Wait!" Aronus called after her. "What about Joe? Do you think he'll follow the map?"

"Oh he will. And when he gets here. He's dead. He'll go right into the realm of shadows, and then we'll follow him in. We'll kill him dead. It's just as simple as that. Now if you don't mind, I'm going to bed."

"But where am I gonna sleep?" Aronus asked.

"On the floor like any dog," she replied simply. "Good night." And with that, she turned and left.

"Do I even get a blanket?" He called. No reply came. So he laid down on the floor and curled up into the fetal position. He fell asleep cold and shivering.

Chapter 2: Trying To Help

It felt great. Joe was finished with school. All known enemies were dead, and there were no large battles coming up. He lay in his bed staring at the ceiling and thinking. This was going to be the perfect summer. The only thing that threw him off, was the map. The map that the weird woman had given him. The place where the map led didn't look too far away, but he still didn't know who she was, or how she had found him. He wondered what kind of help she needed. She looked and sounded really desperate. Of course, Joe could deny her any help and go about his life preparing for college. But he thought that might be considered offensive to whatever idiot *really* wanted him to use this "gift" that he had been giving.

College. Never really something Joe thought he'd do until just recently. It seemed like when he went back in time, everything had changed, including his attitude. He had actually been *nice* and *courteous* to people in the three weeks since his graduation. He didn't like it but it just seemed right. There was still something deep down inside of him that wanted all of mankind to die out so that he wouldn't have any more problems. But that part was really deep down.

He had thought countless times about the Illurian Hotel, and of the things that he encountered while there. He was really sad that it was gone. But the person who ran it was evil. The person who ran it had betrayed him. So what was he feeling so sad about? He took the map from under his pillow, opened it, and looked it over.

The weird thing was that the map gave directions to where ever it led, from his house. Even the most idiotic person would have to admit that it was a little suspicious. He studied the map for a long time and made his decision. He would follow the map, but not without taking some sort of protection with him. He grabbed the sword from under his bed, shrunk it, dropped it into his pocket and left.

"Where are you going honey?" His mother asked him as he stepped into the kitchen.

"I'm going out for a little while mom," he said, and left without another word.

He walked the mile and a half to where the map said *entrance*. But there was nothing here but woods. Against his better judgment, Joe walked into the woods. As soon as he walked in the smell of rotten fish hit him. His eyes watered the stench was so strong.

He went on.

About a mile in, Joe saw a cave. "Man, I hate caves," he said to himself and stepped inside. The cave appeared to be empty. He looked all around and still saw nothing. Then there were two doors on opposite sides of what Joe guessed was a hall. He didn't like choosing doors, but he did it anyway. He dropped the map on the floor and opened and stepped through the door on his left.

"Just go away!" Julya shouted at Aronus. She walked out from her room with a towel wrapped around her head. Aronus followed closely behind her.

"All I want is a shower!" he shouted.

"I told you, you're not good enough for a shower." Aronus stepped on Joe's discarded map and picked it up. He then noticed the open door. "Hey super bitch. You said you gave Joe a map right?"

"Yeah," she said in an annoyed voice.

"One like this?" He waved the map. She walked up and snatched it from him. She looked over it and then at the open door.

"He's gone through you ignoramus." She said. She ripped the towel from her head. "Let's go", she ordered and stepped through the doorway.

"Don't order me around," Aronus said and followed her through. The door slammed shut and collapsed behind him.

Chapter 3: Demon Experiments

This was like no place Joe had ever seen before. The buildings were ridiculously tall. There was trash littering the street, and there was no one at all out and about like normal people would be at this time of the day.

"Hello," he called out, but no one answered. He walked forward to explore this strange new place. It would have been perfectly understandable if the people had merely parked their cars and then disappeared. But there weren't even any cars in this place, at least not that he could see.

Just as Joe turned the corner on the edge of the street, Julya and Aronus came through the door. As soon as Aronus stepped through, the door slammed shut and both of them turned in time to see the door collapse inside of itself.

"You idiot!" Julya screamed. "Who the hell told you to shut the door? Now we're going to be trapped here. Thanks a lot spaghetti for brains."

"Shut up," Aronus said. "There's one way to get back but it's going to take a long time."

"Oh yeah? What way is that?"

"Through the Illurian Hotel. Inside is a portal. Halfway through, the Portal breaks into parts and sends whoever is inside to their respective world", Aronus told her.

"Oh yeah? Give me one good reason why I should believe you."

"It's the only way you're getting home anytime soon."

"How do I know that you know what you're talking about?"

"Because. That was the one part that I couldn't duplicate when I made mine. I tried for centuries."

"Fine. Whatever. How far is it from here?"

"Far. *Very* far."

"How far we talking?"

"A couple years at least."

"You're crazy."

"No I'm not. I know what I'm talking about. Now I'm going to start my quest. See ya around." And with that, he pushed past Julya and walked away.

"Wait for me!" She shouted and took off after him.

Joe had never seen anything like this place. It was weird. There was no one. Every place that he went was deserted. Even the spiders had left. There were plenty of webs sure, but no spiders. No nothing. That is, until Joe came to an old pit that looked out at least a mile. This was no ordinary pit. Normally, you could see some kind of bottom. But he couldn't even see that. He looked down and there was nothing but black, he looked across and could just barely see land. Then he heard a rumbling from deep within the pit. Then there was something that sounded like scurrying. Out of pure instinct, Joe backed away from the pit. And just in time too.

Something came crawling out of the pit on at least a thousand legs. Something that Joe had never seen before. It looked like a cross between an anaconda and a millipede. Joe's eyes widened in terror as the creature came closer.

"Speak your name outlander," the creature said in a deep booming voice. "Speak your name or perish!" Joe thought about it. He didn't want to give his real name to this creature (Miliconda he had decided to call it). So he made one up.

"Jack, Jack Fuchsia," Joe said.

"Son of…"

"Excuse me?"

"Insolent human! Who is your father?!" The creature asked, enraged.

"Umm… Alex Fuchsia." Joe looked the Miliconda in the eye for a moment. The creature only stared back.

"Why do you wish to cross the pit of darkness"

"Someone asked me for my help. The map led into this world but no further. I figured whoever it is must be over there."

"Your figuring is incorrect Human. No one has crossed this pit in over a million years. So go away and allow me to return to my rest. Besides, the only thing that lies beyond this place is Wastelands. Wastelands and the Illurian Hotel." It said.

"Wastelands and the what?"

"Wastelands and the Illurian Hotel."

"That's impossible. I destroyed the Illurian Hotel." Joe said, now very confused.

"Nonsense. No mortal could possibly destroy such a place of power. You must be referring to the rip off created by the Lowest Of The Low. What world do you come from?"

"Earth." Joe said.

"Do you intend to take up residence here?"

"Of course not. Why?"

"Because my senses tell me that all portals in and out of this world have been destroyed. Except the greatest portal of them all. The portal at the Illurian Hotel."

"At that portal, it can get me out of here?" Joe asked.

"Of course. That portal leads into all worlds. To wherever the person wants to go in his or her respective world." The creature told him.

"I used a portal to get here. And I left it open."

"And then two others entered after you. And one of them was The Lowest Of The Low. He closed the portal. And it does not open from this side."

"Impossible. I killed him." Joe said.

"He has been given a second chance to kill you. Him and his assistant are on their way to this very spot at this very moment."

"Are you serious?" Joe asked him in disbelief.

"Of course I am. I am always serious. And never wrong. And that being said The Lowest Of The Low should be here in 5…4…3…2…" Joe turned around and sure enough saw Aronus heading towards him. With a sexy woman dressed in leather following close behind.

Aronus looked up and saw Joe standing in their path. Then he looked to the left of Joe and saw a giant creature standing behind him. "Well well well. Look who's about to die."

"I killed you once, I can do it again." Joe said through gritted teeth. Memories came to him. Things that he didn't *want* to remember. He then looked to the person standing next to Aronus. "You…" He said. This was the woman. The one ho gave him the map, the one who brought him here. He felt a fresh rising of hatred surging through his body.

"Me." Julya said smiling. Joe pulled the sword from his pocket. He enlarged it and put his had down by his side. Julya gasped. "So it does exist." She breathed.

"Of course it exists you ninny." Aronus said. Julya slapped him and left a large red handprint on the side of his face.

"If you ever call me that again, I will rip you skin from your body and use it to redecorate my house. There's sure as hell enough of it." She said.

"Well at least I'm not a bulimic looking assassin who has to pose as a dominatrix just to get someone to look at me." Julya gasped in horror at this.

"Now look here you fat pig, you would do well to remember who the boss is. And right now, we're supposed to be fighting him. Remember?"

"Right."

"The old ones gave you something to destroy him right?"

"Yeah." He began rummaging around in his pocket and pulled out the seven blue cubes. He threw them all into the air. *"Activate!"* He bellowed. The cubes glowed bright green and then began expanding. Seven blinding flashes of light, then the oddest creatures Joe had ever seen were standing in front of them. All of them had eyes as black as night and six arms. But each was distinctly different. 001 was Yellow and at least 15 feet tall. Inside its mouth were at least two-dozen rows of razor sharp teeth made for grinding bones to dust. 045 was as tall as 001, puke green with a small opening on his forehead. The hole opened a portal that lead directly into hell itself. 214 was 10 feet tall with a pinkish skin color. He had a second set of eyes, which hypnotized you into thinking that you were dead and you ended up dying eventually anyway. 587 was at least 20 feet tall (as far as Joe could see). He had black skin so his eyes blended into the skin. This one's eyes had the power to devour your soul, an act that would cause you to spontaneously combust. 599 was 17 feet tall and had a bright white skin. One touch could burn the skin right from your body. 648 was 16 feet tall and had blue skin. This one could put you to sleep with a single look from its eyes, then it would devour you whole. 666 was the smallest of the all.

He was only 2 ½ feet tall with bright red skin. This one was the most diabolical of them all. It could do everything the other's could, plus turn into a human in order to deceive its prey.

All of the creatures except for 001 took to the sky and flew in six different directions.

"**NO!**" The Miliconda shouted. 001 meanwhile bent down, lifted Aronus and Julya and tossed them into his mouth. Suddenly the sound of chainsaw arose. This sound in actuality was the sound of his teeth going into motion. Aronus and Julya's screams were drowned out by this sound but Joe could imagine the pain that they must be in, but he could seem to bring himself to care. After a moment or two the sound stopped. 001 then bent down and spit the dust from his mouth. Then he rounded on Joe. Joe's eyes widened as he realized what was getting ready to happen. He couldn't get away before 001 picked him up and tossed him into his mouth.

Chapter 4: The First Key

Joe didn't like this. It smelled like death in here. Rotting, decaying, moldy death. Then he remembered that he had to move fast. He ran forward dodging through the rows of razor sharp teeth. The only thing slowing him down was this horrible creature's smell, and its spit, which now completely covered his shoes. He managed to clear the teeth before they started to move but when they did Joe had to cover his ears. The sound was deafening. It was like a thousand bees were buzzing around and trying to tear into his head. He looked around for some way out, but saw only one. "You've got to be kidding me." Joe said to himself. The only way out of this place was to go down the creature's throat. It was a long shot, but it was better than being up here with that sound. So he jumped. He fell for a long time but then land on something extra slimy. He felt around and grabbed the sword and held it firmly in his hand. He had an idea. He pointed the sword at the wall opposite him. *"Ignite!"* He bellowed and a great jet of fire shot from the sword's edge and collided with the wall. The whole thing was instantly engulfed in flames. The flames shot up and down the wall. Joe looked up and saw the fire coming down the wall behind him. He turned around and used the sword to cut a hole through the wall. This was surprisingly easy and Joe could see the outside. He looked up again and saw the fire only a few feet above his head.

Joe jumped through the hole and found himself tumbling down the rest of the creature's body. At least he was out of that stench. He landed on the ground with a loud hard **THUD**. He got up and limped quickly away from the beast that was slowly burning up from the inside. He got next to the Miliconda and crouched down behind it. A moment later he heard a deafening shriek and looked up in time to see the creature explode.

When Joe could see properly without spots in front of his eyes, he limped over to where the creature had once been. Floating a few feet above the ground, surrounded in a white light, was a key. This key was sliver and easily the size of a sword. Joe reached in and grabbed it. He felt new power surge through his body.

"What is this thing?" he asked the Miliconda.

"*That*, is one of the seven sacred keys required to enter the Illurian Hotel. " It said.

"Ok. Now what was that thing?"

"One of the guardians of the keys. The key was hidden inside of seven very special warrior demons. I don't think that the people who gave The Lowest Of The Low those cubes knew which one's they were."

"So I have to find all of those things before I can get into the building?" Joe asked.

"Yup."

"Give me a ride?" Joe asked uncertainly.

"Positively not!" The creature said, offended that he would ask such a thing.

"Come one. You'll get to see the world, get out of that stuffy pit. And you said yourself, the only portal left in or out of this world is at the Illurian Hotel. So you won't have many guests unless you come with." Joe said, giving the creature the puppy dogface.

"Oh fine!" The creature gave in. "My name is Lenthral, and if you do one thing that deem offensive, I'll drop you into the ocean. Understood?"

"Yes sir!" Joe said, relieved that he didn't have to walk however far it was to the *real* Illurian Hotel. "It's very nice to meet you Lenthral. My real name is Joe", Joe said taking one of Lenthral's many legs in his hand and shaking it.

"Hop on", Lenthral said and bent down to allow Joe onto his back. Joe climbed up and no sooner had he gotten on proper, Lenthral took off and flew through the sky. The wind felt good blowing through Joe's hair. "By the way. I knew you were lying about your name at first."

"You did not." Joe said.

"I did so." Lenthral told him.

"How'd you know?" Joe asked.

"I always know when someone is lying. And liar was written all over your face. You really should work on that."

"Yeah I should." Joe pondered this as they flew on to find the second of the seven keys. And of course, The Illurian Hotel. At that moment he knew. There would never be anyone else like him. He was Big Joe. The One And Only.

BOOK 2:

RES PUTAR

Chapter 1: The House On ShadowBird Lane

ONE

Joe rode on the back of the Miliconda (half millipede, half anaconda), chasing the demons through the world. There were four suns in this world, and every one of them was beating down on him like a cleaver coming down on a pound of un-tenderized meat. There was one in front of him, on either side, and in back of him, so there was nowhere he could turn to protect himself.

The two of them had been traveling for over a week and had only seen one body of water. The water was a sparkling, clear blue, the color of the sky on a bright spring day. He would have stopped and gotten a drink, but the fish in the water were glowing a disturbingly bright shade of green. So they moved on.

On the ninth day of their travel (Joe was near the point of death from de-hydration), they stopped in front of a large cottage. "I thought you said that there were only wastelands over here," Joe rasped out. His throat was so dry it almost pained him to speak.

"No, I said that there were only wastelands and the Illurian Hotel. This is a part of the wastelands. There are leftover houses everywhere."

"So… if this is a part of the wastelands, then why did we stop?"

"Because, stupid humans tend to leave things behind. Water and other useful things."

"Water," Joe said sarcastically, ignoring the scratching feeling in his throat. "That water can't possibly be any good by now."

"That's the difference between this world and your rinky dinky one. Water over here, it lasts forever."

"Right…" Joe trailed off.

"Are you just gonna sit there like writing on a page all day, or are you going in?" Joe hopped off the miliconda's back and walked slowly up the stairs. He twisted the knob and opened the door.

They both went inside.

TWO

Despite its look from the outside, the inside of this cottage was small and dark. Joe didn't know how, but he could sense the loneliness of the place. The farther inside they went, the more the darkness seemed to move. The more it shifted all around them.

He felt along the walls for a light switch, but he couldn't find one. So he did the next most logical thing. He thought for a moment, and then, "Wrong is wrong and right is right, fill this house with summer's light." A large sun appeared close to the ceiling, bathing the room in artificial sunlight.

"You come up with some of the dumbest spells," the Miliconda said.

"They may be dumb, but at least they work."

"And if the house burns down, then what?"

"The house won't burn down, it's an artificial sun. It'll follow us until I extinguish it."

"And how do you know how to extinguish it?"

"Because I created it." And he walked on. The Miliconda gave a small grunt and followed after him.

THREE

The two of them explored the cottage from top to bottom. The attic (along with the two floors beneath it) held nothing of real value. The most useful thing that they found was a chest filled with daggers. Joe shrunk it, pocketed it and moved on. The real find, was in the basement.

They walked slowly down the stairs, the artificial sun bobbing merrily behind them. The basement was bare, except for a door standing against the opposite wall. Joe walked toward the door and the Miliconda followed.

Inscribed upon this door was a language the likes of which Joe had never seen before.

◆🌢🖐✌☝🏵♁

"Oh come on! Does someone actually expect me to understand this?"

"No. You seem to be forgetting that you're in someone else's house Joe. They obviously understood it and that's all that matters," it said in its snake-like voice. "It says Shadow." Joe looked at him for a moment, then back at the door.

"Then I'm leaving. I don't do too well with shadows," he turned to leave, but the Miliconda blocked his way.

"Open the damn door," it hissed at him.

Joe backed against the door and felt for a knob. He found it and twisted. The knob turned easily and the door opened. He felt a rush of cold air and started sliding downward.

He managed to get turned around and saw that he was indeed going down what appeared to be a large stone sliding board. He hit the bottom in seconds. When he looked back up, he could no longer see the door. He looked around the dark room and realized that the sun had gone out. As he started to say the spell to re-ignite it, Lenthral and the original, still burning, artificial sun came sliding down.

Now that there was light, Joe could see a chest at the far end of the room. He walked forward and stopped. He knelt down and read what was inscribed on the Chest. **JOE.**

He opened the chest. Inside was a large, leather bound book. The book was black and encrusted with jewels and gems. On it, in golden letters was, **Le Livre De Vie.** Joe picked it up and opened it to the first page behind the cover. It bared the book's title once again. "This book has to be a thousand pages long," Joe said. He opened to the next page and there was nothing.

He flipped through the pages and found some very interesting things. But that's not for now. Also in the chest, Joe saw when he looked back down, were bottles and bottles of water. A large smile spread across Joe's face and he grabbed a bottle tore off the top, and drunk it down in three gulps. He did this with six more bottles. The water was never ending. Every time he opened a bottle, another one appeared.

Once his thirst was quenched, he put the book back on top of the remaining bottles and closed the chest. "*Shrink!*" He said and the chest obeyed his command, shrinking to the size of a walnut. Joe picked it up and put it in his pocket. "So um… how do we get upstairs?" Joe asked, looking around the room. The Miliconda sighed.

"Open the door, you twit."

"Ok, you know what Lenthral? I'm getting tired of you talking down to me."

The stop acting like a rambling idiot."

"You know what? This is your world, not mine. It's gonna take a while for me to catch up." Joe said and went to the door. He opened the door and within seconds he was being sucked upwards. Then came Lenthral. They exited the basement and went to the front door.

"*Extinguish!*"

The sun went out.

FOUR

Joe rode the back of the Miliconda for the next three hours, still thumbing through the book. He found all sorts of incantations and ingredients for different kinds of potions. He also found a section on demons. This was, by far the most interesting. He didn't finish reading it, but what he did finish was very informative. But Joe could write his own spells, and he had never used potions before. There *was* one extremely interesting incantation, however.

Across the top of the page, it read: LARAL NANTU SIENTO. The rest of the page was in English, but this one particular phrase jumped out at him. "Laral Nantu Siento," Joe said aloud. "What does that mean?"

"It means: Bring To Power," Lenthral said without looking up. He (it) stared straight ahead, watching the skies like a hawk for any sign of danger.

Joe looked back to the book and red the spell aloud. "Hail to the powers of the light towers to the north, the beginning of all known dear. Hail to the powers of the dark towers to the south, at the beginning and center of fear. North to south, east to west, aid me in forever's test.

The powers are yours, yet let them be mine, so that our life forces may be intertwined." The words glowed and vanished, and a strong wind began to blow.

Joe slammed the book shut and threw himself down onto Lenthral's back. "What did you do?! Stop it you little twit!" The Miliconda shouted over the eardrum shattering wind.

"**I CAN'T!!**" Joe shouted back. He held on for fear life, digging his nails into the Miliconda's scales. The book pressed uncomfortably into his chest, but he didn't want to risk shrinking it.

The wind became a gust as things were picked up from the ground. Joe slowly lifted his head (considering the force of the gust, this was no easy feat), and his mouth dropped open in horror. In front of them was a large white tornado. Out of instinct alone, Joe turned around (again, no easy feat), and as he expected, there was a large black tornado.

He went back to his original position and pressed his face against the scales of Lenthral.

Seconds later, both tornados closed in like eagles swooping down on prey, and collided. Joe and the Miliconda still in between them.

FIVE

Ten minutes later, Joe woke up. He was dizzy, floating, and glowing. He sat up and looked around. He saw white and black orbs swirling around him. That didn't bother him too much. He only panicked when he noticed that he was floating. He gave a small yelp and fell to the ground. He sat up and rubbed his temple, temporarily interrupting the band of orbs settled there. Finally, the orbs subsided.

Joe stood up and turned around, only to come face to face with Lenthral, eyes wide and teeth bared like a rabid dog preparing to attack. "Next time you try to kill me because we had a disagreement," it hissed.

"Stab me like a normal person would. Don't try to get me sucked up by tornados. Especially with you still on me."

"I didn't know that would happen, honest! I just said the spell and then that happened. I think… I think that it was the forces of the towers combining with me." Joe said, screwing up his face in puzzlement.

" A likely story."

"No. There was another one behind us. That one was black. That last part of the spell. 'The Powers are yours, yet let them be mine, so that our life forces may be intertwined.' Our three sets of powers really became intertwined with one another."

"I think I would have felt it if a tornado was riding up on our ass!" The Miliconda said, eyes now tiny slits in its head.

"Fine. If you don't wanna believe me, don't. But don't try to tell me what I saw. I know that I saw a second tornado back there! I'm not crazy!"

"I, I, I," The Miliconda mocked. "Will you stop whining and complaining like a little girl already? You screwed up. Just admit it and stop trying to blame it on someone else."

"Will you just shut up already!?!" Joe shouted. Lenthral's eyes widened in terror. The entire back half of his (its) body erupted in flames. He (it) let out a shrill cry of pain and began running around the field. The flames licked at his (its) scales and they peeled off one by one.

"Jacko Amparticus!" He (it) screamed. "You'll never reach the hotel alive!" And then he (it) exploded, snake guts and blood splattering all over the field.

Joe surveyed the ground with a feeling of despair washing over him. He wasn't sure how, but he had just destroyed his ride through this strange and desolate world. And then everything changed.

The barren wastelands that made up this world, became lush green fields of grass and flowers. The dust-filled brown cloudy sky, became a clear cloudless blue. And three of the four suns vanished. Pools of beautiful, crystal clear water appeared in the fields and Joe could feel them popping up all over the world.

Joe looked from coast to coast, taking in the now beautiful scenery, then he realized it. The book was gone. He searched frantically for the book, and finally found it under Lenthral's heart. He reached down and tried to move the heart, but it wouldn't budge. Then it started beating.

Joe stepped back and looked at the beating heart in terror. The heart started out slow, but then accelerated to an excruciatingly fast pace. And then, without any warning at all, the heart exploded. More blood covered Joe's face.

The book was now completely covered. But (also without warning) the book absorbed the blood and flew open. It flipped to nearly the back, where Joe had not had a chance to read yet. The page that it opened to contained some (somewhat) shocking information.

Joe read.

SIX

Lenthral Losomener is one of the last remaining demons that possess true power enough to do anything more than conjure a table. He also possesses great strength. No one knows exactly what Lenthral is. The only thing that anyone knows for certain, is that anyone in their right mind would not go up against him. He once ripped twenty-seven people limb from limb in less that a minute.

His eyes secrete a strange fluid that if touched directly, will burn the skin from your very bones and leave behind nothing but a screaming, blithering skeleton.

This particular demon is known best for his powers of persuasion and his glamour techniques. It is recorded that he once created a glamour that caused fifty people to rob a museum in order to steal the precious four-point diamond. Apparently they believed that they were being instructed by their king.

Perhaps his most deadly ability of all, is the ability to change the landscape to fit his own needs and/or desires. This can be to ensure his own safety, and to endanger the life of his adversary.

The only known weaknesses are grass, and flowers. Get these ingredients and mix them in with plain, natural tap water and you may have a CHANCE of defeating him. That is, of course, if he doesn't incinerate you first. Once destroyed, all changes that Lenthral made, will be undone. But what's the point really? If he's not after you then you could be living in a paradise.

SEVEN

Joe found the last two lines of the page especially stupid and wondered why anyone would put there. But even on top of the stupidity of this particular page, Joe couldn't believe that he had been deceived again. "What is it with me?" He asked himself as he sat on the ground in a small puddle of snake blood. "Do I have 'betray me' written on my forehead or something?" He re-shrank the book then got up, put it in his pocket and began to walk. Momentarily, he thought of conjuring something to ride on or in, but he needed the walk to clear his mind and think about Lenthral, the demons, and his next plan to get to the portal, so decided against it.

He walked for at least six hours, stopping only to sit down and rest or take a swim in one of the newly formed ponds. Once he got tired of the water and felt refreshed, he got up and resumed his journey.

After a while, he came to another abandoned house. By this time, it was dark outside and Joe could hardly see anything in front of him. Though he could make out what appeared to be a street sign that said SHADOWBIRD LANE. He walked up the stairs and entered the house.

This house was considerably different from the cottage that he had seen earlier in the day. For one thing, the electricity (oddly enough) still worked. As soon as Joe stepped into the front room of the house, light poured from beneath the lampshades and flooded the room. Joe walked up the fairly large flight of stairs to the first door on his right. He opened the door and saw an enormously comfortable looking queen sized bed. And then the clock struck twelve, and the door slammed shut. "Oh come on!" Joe shouted and threw the door open again.

Staring back at him was what appeared to be some kind of wormhole. The edges were dark blue, and the center was black and crackling with electricity. He figured out what was about to happen and immediately tried to shut the door, but was too late and was sucked in.

EIGHT

Joe stood up groggily and rubbed his head. *I hate this world.* He thought to himself as he stumbled forward. The room (or wherever he was) was bathed in dark blue light. When he was able to walk normally again, he looked up and was stopped dead in his tracks. In front of him was a vision so beautiful and so divine that it made him fall to his knees and stare up at it. In front of him was a chained girl with darkish brown hair. Her eyes were a dazzling shade of green. "Thank God!" She gasped out, looking down at him. This girl couldn't have been any older than Joe himself, so how did she get to be so beautiful?

Joe slowly stood up, feeling like a love-struck teenage girl. "So... so... so pretty," he managed to stutter out. She smiled. Her teeth were a brilliant shade of white, and Joe was literally blinded for a moment. The only thing that wasn't drop-dead, stunningly gorgeous on this girl, was her clothes. Her clothes consisted of nothing more than tattered rags covering (just barely) the most essential parts of her body. Finally his eyes registered this little fact and he thought to himself, *What if she doesn't want to be seen like this?* Joe was going to choose this time to test out his new powers, if he hadn't felt something dropping in his pocket. He reached in and pulled out the chest, which was the only thing in that pocket.

He put it down on the ground and enlarged it. Opening it up revealed not bottles of water like it had the previous time. But instead, one blue jean outfit complete with long-sleeve black t-shit, and a pair of beige cargo pants with a sleeveless camouflage shirt. Before Joe could say a word, both outfits vanished from the chest and fulfilled their new owners need for clothes. The chest closed. Joe re-shrunk it and dropped it in his pocket.

"Thanks," the girl said. "But now we have to get out of here. Before Hell head comes back."

"Before *who* comes back?" He saw fear in her eyes as she looked past him and her eyes traveled slowly upward. Joe turned around and came face-to-face (in a manner of speaking) with Demon Experiment number 045. Puke green and fifteen feet tall with that black hole in the middle of its forehead.

"Oh crap," Joe gasped. "Why didn't you tell me that you were under guard by 045?" He called over his shoulder.

"I didn't know. I just call it Hell head because of that thing in its head. It opens a portal that sends you directly into the pits of hell."

"Is that really what it does?" Joe whimpered under his breath. Then, he did the only thing he could think of. He pulled the sword from his pocket and enlarged it.

The hole in the middle of 045's head began to glow a bright red and it let out a mighty roar. A beam shot from the hole and directly at Joe. He deflected it with the sword and attacked, not paying any attention to the red/black portal that opened on one of the walls.

He drove the sword deep into the demon's foot and it let out a deafening shriek. It bent down and swiped at him. He rolled out of the way and over to the girl. Every visible inch of her milky skin seemed to glow with the light from the portal. Joe looked up and saw the demon coming towards him again, and used the sword's immense power to cut the chains binding the girl. Her arms dropped and she rubbed at her wrists.

Joe rolled back into battle, swiping at what he could reach. And then the unthinkable happened. His vision eye opened and shot its beam and made its screen. The vision was this: Joe, the girl, and another boy that Joe had seen once before. The three of them were standing in what appeared to be a pumpkin patch. All of them were staring at something, mouths hanging open and eye sparkling. The screen vanished when Joe was swatted against the nearest wall by 045's claw. "No!" He heard the girl scream.

Joe was immobilized for a moment, blood trickling down his forehead. He found himself in a daze. He was brought back to his senses by the girl's frantic screams for help. "Let go of her you bastard!" A voice came from over by the portal.

Joe's vision cleared and he saw the boy from his vision climbing up 045's leg. And then he looked back at Joe. "Go for the head!" He shouted and continued climbing. Joe looked up and realized that it wasn't a hole in the middle of 045's head. It was a gem. One of those weird magical stones you always hear about on T.V. So he got up, and ran towards the demon's foot. He jumped up, landed on the foot, and used it for leverage in jumping the rest of the way. He surpassed the boy and drove the sword into the demon's leg to avoid falling. He grabbed onto a scale and pulled himself up, wrenching the sword out of the demon flesh and back into it above his head. He continued this pattern until he reached the top, the poor boy still below him getting drenched in green and black blood.

Joe reached the top of the demon's head, raised the sword high in the air, and drove it deep into the now glowing gem. There was a flash of red light. 045 gave one final, deafening roar, and keeled over backwards. The demon dissolved, and Joe (along with the other brown boy) hit the ground with a *thud*. Floating a few feet above the ground where the heart should have been, was the second key to the Illurian Hotel.

This key, like the first, was easily the size of a sword. The only difference was that this one was solid gold. Joe grabbed the key and felt another new surge of power. He shrunk it and put it in his pocket. The girl stepped forward. "Thank you," she said. "My name's Stephanie. Stephanie Danielson." She extended her hand. He shook it.

"I'm Joseph Austin."

"And I'm Adrian Gibbs", the boy said. He also extended his hand.

"Um… hi." Joe said and reluctantly shook his hand. The demon blood was warm, shiny, and sticky. Their two hands stuck together for a moment.

This boy was roughly 5' 8" with short hair and slightly muscular. His eyes were a dark brown and his skin was the shade of chocolate milk.

There was another effect of the blood. It caused what clothes he was wearing to shrink-to-fit. He bent forward to stretch and Stephanie bit her lip, suppressing a scream. When he stood straight again, he could feel her eyes traveling down his backside, taking in every inch. Then he turned around, and she saw the way his skin glistened. She started to sweat, and her eyes went downward again. She got halfway down, took in a sharp gasp, and fled from the room, through the portal into the house. He looked to Joe and then down at himself.

"What the hell???" he shouted. His body was covered in leeches, each one chewing its way inside. Halfway down was a rather large one, slithering its way upward. On his backside, there were maggots crawling everywhere. "Shit! Shit! Shit!" He started trying to swat them off.

"Stand still!" Joe shouted. He pointed the sword at one of the leeches. This was risky, but he had to try. *"Petrinolious!"* Joe shouted and the leech froze. All the others and the maggots followed. Each shattered and fell off one by one. "Sorry 'bout that. I'm still new at the whole fighting demons thing. No one told me that their blood was full of critters." Joe looked slightly embarrassed.

"No one ever told me either. But then again, no one I know believes in demons or anything like that." They stood silent for a moment. "Maybe we should find Stephanie."

"Yeah," Joe said, and led the way through the portal back into the house.

NINE

The door slammed shut behind them, causing a rippling effect of doors slamming all down the hall. "Um... I'll look for Stephanie. *You* might wanna take a shower." Joe said.

"Right," Adrian said. "Uh, where's the bathroom?"

"I don't know." Adrian nodded and disappeared down the hall. Joe thought for a second, and then re-opened the door. Once again, there was the queen sized enormously comfortable looking bed. There was no Stephanie, however, so he moved on.

Seven doors down he found her, sitting on the bed rocking back and forth, babbling to her self. "Stephanie… are you ok?" Joe asked cautiously.

"Leeches…maggots…demons…what did I do to deserve this?" She was almost in tears. "I was a good kid. Always did my work in school. I even directed a play. And then I get sucked in here." A single tear fell from here eye. The tear dripped from her chin and onto the bed beneath her. The bed glowed and floated a little off of the floor. Stephanie's hair raised itself up so that her forehead was visible. And on her forehead appeared a glowing mark. It was (what appeared to be) Joe's initials. (The way he wrote them anyway.) An odd sort of $\mathcal{JA}$. The bed stopped floating and her hair laid flat. Everything stopped glowing too. Joe's initials vanished from her forehead.

"What just happened?" She asked.

"I think you're supposed to come with me," Joe said.

"Come with you where? I don't even know you that well."

"The reason I'm here, I got trapped in this world. Now I'm looking for this place called the Illurian Hotel. It's got the only portal back home. So I have to find it."

"I'll come with you!" She said quickly. "Anything to get out of this place."

"Ok. We'll leave in the morning." He turned to leave.

"Wait!" Joe turned back around. " What about Adrian? We can't just leave him here."

"I know that. We'll take him with us."

"Good." She smiled. "He's too cute to leave behind."

"That's the only reason you want to take him with us? So you can *look* at him?" Joe looked at her in disbelief.

"Well…he *is* easy on the eyes. And he's funny and sweet and–" She was cut off by a yell from down the hall. Stephanie jumped off the bed and raced out of the room, Joe close behind her.

When they reached the room they believed the yell had originated in, they threw open the door and saw Adrian standing on the toilet wearing only a towel. "What the hell is wrong with you?" Joe asked, ignoring Stephanie's tightening grip on his arm.

"The fucking floor is crawling!" He said. Joe looked down at the floor and saw that the floor was indeed crawling. It appeared to be infested with maggots and other little white creatures that looked oddly like freshly emerged cicadas.

"Why'd you come in here if the floor was crawling?"

"I didn't. I got out of the shower and just started feeling stuff crawling over my foot." He saw the look of disbelief on Joe's face. "Just get rid of them!"

"No. *You* get rid of them." Joe took the sword from his pocket, enlarged it, and tossed it to Adrian. Instantly, the sword's golden blade began to glow. And then Joe's glowing initials appeared on Adrian's head. But another mark appeared too. This one was two snakes, coiled around each other. Joe suddenly found himself remembering something he had read. This mark, it was called the mark of the warrior. And then the glowing stopped and the marks vanished.

"What the hell just happened?" Adrian asked.

"I'll explain it later. Right now, just get rid of these things. And put some clothes on." Joe closed the door and walked off up the hallway, Stephanie following close behind him.

TEN

"There's something's wrong with this house," Joe said, plopping down on the bed once he and Stephanie were back in the room. She sat down next to him. "I can feel it. Something happened here. Something so horrible, that whoever or whatever it happened to is still trapped here."

"How can you be sure?"

"I don't know. It's just a feeling really."

"Are you going to help it?"

"No. This thing, whatever it is, is beyond help. Too much has happened. It's too angry."

"What's too angry?" Adrian asked, appearing in the doorway. He threw the sword to Joe. Joe put it on the floor.

"Joe thinks the house is haunted."

"Haunted? A ghost? In this house?" He asked sarcastically. "Get outta—"

"Not a ghost," Joe said. "A poltergeist." He looked at the both of them, prepared to let his guard down and accept them as equals. For now. " We have to get out of here. Not tomorrow, not in an hour. Now. Before our spirit friend decides that it wants company for the next century. So let's go." Joe thought for a moment. "Adrian...where did you get those clothes?"

"Out of one of the dressers up the hall."

Joe turned around. "Take 'em off."

"What?"

"The clothes, take them off."

"Are you insane?" He asked. "I have nothing else to put on."

"I'll find you something. Just get out of those clothes."

"Fine. Whatever." He tried to pull the shirt off, but it wouldn't come over his head. "Um…is it just me, or is it getting harder to breathe in here?" Joe turned back around and walked over. Upon closer inspection, Joe could see that the shirt collar was shrinking around Adrian's neck.

Joe grabbed the sword from the floor and placed it on the collar of the shirt. It split instantly and fell to the floor. He tossed the sword to Stephanie.

"What's this for? She asked, obviously confused.

"Cut the pants. Waist to crotch and down the rest of the way. And… uh…be mindful of the…you know." A look of realization dawned on her face and she nodded. Joe turned back around.

After a few seconds, Joe heard the sound of ripping denim. Then, seconds later, "Damn it! Watch where you're cutting with that thing Steph! I'd actually like to be able to make children when I'm older."

There was a mumbled "Sorry," and then more ripping fabric. A moment later, "Done!" Joe took the chest from his pocket, put it on the floor and enlarged it. Stephanie kicked it open and Joe heard what sounded suspiciously like wind chimes. He turned around and saw Adrian standing there with blue jeans and a black t-shirt. The chest also supplied him with shoes. Joe closed the chest, shrunk it and put it back in his pocket. Stephanie handed him the sword, which he also shrunk and dropped into his pocket.

"Ok. Now we really need to get out of here." Joe said. "Let's go."

They left the room quickly and proceeded down the stairs. Joe reached the door first and realized that it would not open. "What's going on?!" Stephanie asked frantically.

"It doesn't want us to leave," Joe said. "Stand back." The both of them stood back. Joe pulled the sword from his pocket, enlarged it, raised it in the air and brought it down through the door. He pulled it out and saw that it had created a rather large hole. Instantly, the door healed itself. Then Joe felt something. It was almost as if he were being sucked backwards. He looked back and saw large green floating semi-transparent head, sucking in air, trying to keep them captive. He pushed Stephanie and Adrian to one side of the door and he moved to the other. Just as he planned, the door was sucked inward and hit this thing in the head. The sucking stopped and the three of them ran from the house. Joe turned back at the bottom of the steps outside and put the sword to it. *"Ignite!"* He shouted and a jet of fire poured forth from the tip of the sword, setting the house ablaze.

Joe darted forward and took cover. He could hear the house shrieking as it burned. Within seconds the house burned to the ground, but the poltergeist within it still shrieked. As the sun began to creep into the sky, the tortured creature within the house gave one, final deafening roar, and then there was silence.

ELEVEN

The three of them walked till midday, then slept for three hours, and then walked on until sundown. They pitched camp near a wooded area, and all three were glad that the house on ShadowBird Lane was behind them.

CHAPTER 2: THE WINTER WONDERLAND

ONE

The three of them went on for a week and a half before they encountered another demon. In that week, Adrian Gibbs experienced more bad luck than ever in his life. First, he slid down a muddy slope on a perfectly clear day. At the bottom of this slope, was a small lake crawling with poisonous water snakes. Then there was the time that he was practicing his magic with Joe. Joe was teaching him how to throw fireballs (which he had no business doing, considering he was just learning himself), and one of them ricocheted off of a stone mountain, nearly incinerating him. (Luckily, he knew how to duck, so what little hair he had growing was only partially singed.

The next day there was a meteor shower. He was hit with several of them. The last, and perhaps most traumatizing experience, came in the form of a twenty-foot-long catfish who mistook his shoelace for a worm. The thing clamped down on his entire foot and dragged him into the lake. There, (even after the fish realized that it had a human instead of a worm.) it tried to devour him. It would have bitten him in half if Joe hadn't jumped in and saved him.

But once they met demon experiment number 214, everything changed for Adrian. And it changed with something as simple as a kiss.

TWO

After the catfish incident, all three of them decided to stay away from water if they could manage it. The only time they went near water was to bathe, and occasionally wash their outfit. Every so often, they would pass a village, but after what happened with the last house, they weren't in any hurry to spend the night in a house uninvited. So they camped, night after night. It was during one of these campings that they had a certain conversation.

"So what'll happen when we get there? The Illurian Hotel I mean." Stephanie asked after one night after a dinner that consisted of strange blue balls that tasted oddly like bacon.

"We go home." Joe said simply. "Back to our families and friends. Well…friends for you guys at least."

"What do you mean?" Stephanie asked.

"I don't have any friends. I was too evil to people to ever have friends. And then I killed someone. Three someone's actually. Two out of the three, I had grown to trust. But one of them betrayed me, and the other one hurt me. Eventually, all three of them tried to kill me. But I got them first. One of them, it actually hurt to kill. I kinda considered a friend." Joe looked to his two companions, vulnerable and afraid. "I'm trapped in an alien world. To tell the truth, I have no idea how to get where we're going. I'm just guessing and assuming. I don't even know how to find the demons I'm looking for. I need help. I'm not ashamed to admit it anymore. So I'm telling you now. If either of you turns on me, I will kill you - without a moment's hesitation. For right now, I'm considering the two of you as my equals, as my friends. We're at the point right now, where I trust you enough not to roll you over the side of a cliff while you're sleeping. The rest of the trust will build up...eventually. Now I know that this is turning into on of those long drawn out retarded speeches that I always hated. So I'll stop after you answer me this one question. Do you trust me?" The three of them exchanged glances for a moment. Finally, Stephanie nodded, slowly at first, but with more enthusiasm as she continued. Then Adrian joined in. And then they both stopped.

The three of them were silent, and once again, Stephanie spoke up. "Can I see that book you were telling us about?"

"Sure," Joe said, pulling the walnut sized book from his pocket. "*Enlarge!*" He said, and it grew to its actual size. He handed the book over to her.

"Thanks," she said. Then she opened it and started looking through the various pages.

'Joe.' A voice spoke up in his head.

'Who is that?' Joe asked stupidly, and then realized that he was talking (thinking) to nothing more than a figment of his imagination. He continued staring down at the dirt.

'It's me. Adrian.' Joe looked up. Adrian was looking at him.

'You can't throw fireballs without nearly setting yourself on fire, yet you can use advanced telepathy. How is that?'

'Telepathy won't burn me to a cinder.'

'What do you want?' Joe returned his attention to the dirt.

'What are we gonna do with her?'

"What do you mean?"

'She's like one of those damsel in distress characters just waiting to be captured and held for some obscenely high ransom.'

'If and when that time comes, she'll be able to handle it.'

'Joe we have to protect her.'

'That's funny,' Joe thought at him.

'What is?'

'The two of us were talking earlier about how *we're* supposed to protect *you*.'

'Protect me? I don't need anyone to protect me.'

'Really?'

'Really.'

'So I guess you could have handled that huge catfish on your own?'

'My point is, we can't let anything happen to *her*.'

Joe looked up at him. 'You really care abou–"

"Aha!" The both of them looked over at her. "Found something." She handed the book to Joe. At the top of the page in big bold letters it said **DEMON LOCATER.** He looked up at Stephanie. "All you had to was look. Just re-word it and it should be fine." Joe looked at the spell and read it aloud, changing some words here and there.

"Demon experiments far and near, under the watchful gaze of a seer. The five remaining demons which I seek, guide me with something small and sleek." An object appeared in his hand. Smooth and made of glass. It looked like a mini crystal ball. Within the ball was a pinkish demon with a second pair of eyes. Experiment 214. Then it vanished and was replaced by a map. According to the map, 214 was less than ten miles east of them. He looked up at Stephanie. "I hate smart people sometimes," he said with a smirk.

"I do what I can," she said, smiling.

"Ok, this says that the next experiment is less than ten miles from here. In the same direction we've been going."

"And what *is* the next experiment?" Stephanie asked.

"Experiment 214."

"What does it do?" Adrian asked, staring into the fire.

"According to my last ride, it hypnotizes you into thinking that you're dead. So then you start acting like a zombie. Eating brains and flesh, the whole nine yards."

"Gross!" Stephanie said, making a face that only she could make.

"We should get to it sometime tomorrow. Should be fine as long as no one looks it in the eyes.

"Ok...uh...isn't this thing like twenty feet tall?" Adrian asked, finally looking up.

"Seventeen. Roughly. But I'm sure it has its ways." He looked at the both of them. "We don't need to talk about it now. We'll talk while we're walking tomorrow." And with that, he got up and laid down on a bed made of leaves. Adrian and Stephanie did the same with theirs.

"Shouldn't someone put the fire out?" Stephanie asked. Joe snapped his fingers and the fire died down. Then died completely. "I have a question."

"What is it Steph?" Joe asked.

"You've got all this power, so...why can't you conjure us a car or something?"

"I tried," he said matter-of-factly. "When I got in it, it fell apart. Now go to sleep."

Then two of them slept. And the one by the name of Stephanie Danielson lie awake.

THREE

Eventually, Stephanie slept. All three of them slept and dreamt. They dreamt of a field of pumpkins. At the end of which, stood a majestic stone building towering high above the clouds. On this stone in great bold letters was THE ILLURIAN HOTEL. Then this vision was ripped away and replaced by a not-so pleasant one. Thousands of bodies littering the ground. Above the bodies stand (or floats) a large metallic object. Then this one too is ripped away. It is replaced with snow. Nothing but white, slushy snow.

The three of them woke startled.

FOUR

It was promptly 7:45 am when they woke the next morning (according to Joe's watch anyway, though in this world there was honestly no telling), neither one of them remembering a thing about the dream that had vanished from their heads moments ago. Each in turn used the nearby lake to bathe, staying in the shallow end for fear of more giant fish. Then they began their journey. When Joe checked the locator, he saw that 214 was now 12 miles east of them. They walked on.

Fifteen minutes later, they reached a clearing. The walked until they got to the center and Joe stopped abruptly. "What's the matter?" Adrian asked.

"There's something wrong." Joe said, surveying the area.

"What do you mean?" Stephanie asked.

"Don't you feel that? There's the regular heat, but then it's cold too." Joe looked at the two of them. The both looked fully prepared to have him hauled away in a straight jacket. "Steph, stand here," he switched places with her so that she was in the middle. "You feel it don't you?" She stood silent for a moment.

"Whoa," she was mesmerized almost. "What is that?"

"I don't know. But I don't thing it's good. We need to get out of here. Before something—" Joe's last words were drowned out by a great roar from just behind them.

The three of them whirled around immediately and looked upward, expecting to see something towering over everything. There was nothing there. The roar came again, this time causing the ground to quake violently. Joe looked down some and saw a pinkish figure, at very least ten feet tall, obscured by the trees. Adrian and Stephanie caught sight of this also.

"Demon number 214, I presume." Stephanie said.

"You presume correctly." Joe said, not taking his eyes off of the demon.

"What do we do?" Adrian asked.

"Well that's a dumb question. We do the only thing we can do," Joe took the sword from his pocket and enlarged it. "We fight." The two of them looked at him. " Ok fine, *I* fight."

214 emerged into the clearing, all four eyes set on Joe and his companions. "Here we go." A look. "Here *I* go." And he charged, sword raised high above his head. And then he thought to himself. *I am not in a warrior movie.* He lowered the sword partially. He pointed it at 214. "*Ignite!*" Joe shouted and fire flowed from the sword's tip and bounced off of 214's legs. Then the demon opened its mouth and its tongue darted out, and wrapped itself around Stephanie. What happened after that was nearly a blur.

Stephanie screamed at the top of her lungs when 214 "reeled" her in just enough to grab her with its massive hand. It held her up in front of its second set of eyes. She screamed louder when the eyes started to glow a shade of black as dark as a thousand midnights. And then the screaming was done, and 214 threw her. She whizzed right past Adrian and vanished at the spot where the cold met the heat. "No!" Adrian shouted, but before he could dive in after her, 214 had him in its grasp. And its eyes glowed again, and the shouting stopped again, and again this poor young child flew threw the air and vanished where cold and hot mixed.

Joe looked up at demon experiment number 214, his eyes on fire with rage.

The demon's tongue lashed out at him, and instead of rolling out of the way, he cut it off. 214 let out a shriek and Joe was covered in blood. He immediately saw the leeches and the maggots, but he didn't care. He shot the flame again, this time further up, and it hit right between the demon's eyes. It stayed this time, the fire burned wildly.

Joe ran forward and began madly slashing 214's leg. Every inch of skin that he could reach, he slashed it. Then he moved to the other leg. Eventually, Joe could see the demon's leg bone, so he kept on cutting. Then he cut the bone clear in half, and the demon toppled over. The fire by now had consumed most of this creature's head, but its cries drowned out the roar of the flames. Joe hopped up onto the body and made his way to where the heart should have been. He got there and the leeches and maggots instantly dropped off because the flames were so intense. Joe raised the sword and drove it into the demon's chest. Another loud cry. Then Joe jumped off.

He looked at this pitiable creature, destined to die at his hands just as the others were. And for a second, he actually felt sorry for it. It dawned on him. These creatures, all of them were created for destruction and mayhem. They had no greater purpose, so all that awaited them was death. Nothing more, nothing less. By now, the body was completely engulfed in flames, and therefore too bright to stare at any longer.

Then Joe heard a rumbling, and knew what was about to happen. So he ran and tried to take cover, but before he could get more than ten feet away, 214 exploded. The force of the explosion was so intense, it sent Joe flying though the air and into a whole new world.

FIVE

Stephanie landed face down in the snow, followed closely by Adrian. Both pulled themselves up after a moment in the cold white substance. The snow that now covered their faces melted away almost instantly. Both of their faces at the moment were expressionless, and their eyes were completely black.

The two of them surveyed the landscape, taking in every white inch. A unicorn galloped up to the two of them. "My master requests you presence," the unicorn said. Stephanie couldn't take her eyes off of its horn. It was six inches long and appeared to be crafted from solid gold. Its coat was so white, the creature blended in with the snow. "My name is Jellon, please follow me." And then something jumped from a nearby bush and made a swipe at the unicorn. The beautiful white coat quickly became crimson, and the unicorn gasped in pain. Entrails fell from the beautiful creature's side.

Stephanie rushed forward and fell to her knees next to the dead horse-like creature. She picked up one of the crimson objects from the snow and shoved it in her mouth. A look of ecstasy spread across her face. She gobbled the rest of the entrails and then reached inside of the unicorn, searching for more.

While Stephanie feasted, Adrian stood facing the creature that had killed the other one. This thing was dressed in leather pants and a long leather shirt. Its skin was a sickening shade of yellow, and its facial features were horribly distorted. The creature smiled and Adrian instantly saw it for what it was, a vampire, complete with razor sharp claws.

"*My* master requests your presence," the vampire said to him. "Please follow me." As soon as it turned its back, Adrian tackled the creature in the snow. He turned the thing over and ripped a hole in its stomach. He and Stephanie feasted together on the innards of two dead creatures.

As they were eating the flesh, there was a rushing of wind and both took in sharp breaths. They shook their heads and when they opened their eyes again, they were normal. Stephanie looked down at her hand and screamed. She threw the last piece of unicorn flesh to the ground and noticed that she was kneeling next to a large horse skeleton. Adrian threw the few remaining pieces of vampire flesh to the ground and noticed that he was sitting on a human shaped skeleton.

She looked back at him, but before she could say a utter a single syllable, another unicorn swooped down from the sky, grabbed her and took off again, positioning her between its hooves as it flew. "Stephanie!" Adrian shouted, and before he could take off after her, a vampire clawed its way out of the snow, grabbed him, and returned the way that it came.

SIX

Joe landed on something hard and let out a cry in agony. He got up and massaged his lower back. He turned around to see what he had fallen on, and saw (much to his horror) a human skeleton laying face up in the blood red snow. There was another one (this one shaped like a horse) a few feet away, also surrounded by blood red snow. He looked around and as far as he could see, there was only white. New snow started to fall.

Joe heard what sounded like the flapping of wings coming from just above him and looked up. There was nothing there but the sun. Joe looked near it and it felt like his eyes were on fire. He shut his eyes tight and turned his face back in the direction of the snow. He opened his eyes. They watered a little bit, but all in all they would be okay. In the snow, he thought that he could see the slight indentation of a footprint, but he wasn't sure if it was his or not.

Now the snow was coming down harder, and it was piling up past Joe's ankles. He knew that he had to find shelter of some kind, or he would freeze to death.

Joe explored.

SEVEN

The unicorn dropped Stephanie in the middle of what looked like a high-price lawyer's office and took off once again. She looked up, only to be greeted by Adrian's smiling face. He was seated in a large EZ-chair, behind a desk made of the finest hand crafted mahogany.

"Hey Steph," he said. She stood up slowly.

"Adrian…" she said. "It can't be. There's no way that you could have gotten here before I did."

"Of course there's a way," he said. "A really simple explanation for all of this. I set it up." He smiled the way only a maniac could smile. Stephanie looked at him in full-blown disbelief.

No… you can't have. We were together the entire time."

"Not the entire time," he said, still smiling. "Remember when you were being held hostage by that thing in that house? I was plotting. I was warned of our little friend's arrival. He's gonna destroy everything. He's evil." Stephanie stared at him.

"No. That's not true. He- he helped us."

"Then why are we here? If he was helping us, then how did that demon get a hold of us? He doesn't give a damn about either one of us. We're in this alone. Did you honestly believe all that crap about him trusting us? About him 'counting us as equals'? If you did…then you're not the smart girl that I thought you were." He looked at her, his face now completely expressionless.

"I'm so confused," she said. "I don't know *who* to believe."

"Believe *me*," he said. "I wouldn't lie to you." He extended his arms. "Come here," he beckoned. She walked slowly towards him, and then sat on his lap. He closed his arms around her. "Now listen," and he whispered in her ear, great and terrible things. She nodded in understanding and he whispered more.

On the other end of this strange wintery world, the same thing was happening. Except it was the other way around. The *real* Adrian was sitting on Stephanie's lap and she was whispering into his ear, and he was nodding in understanding.

They both understood.

EIGHT

Joe walked for ages, but saw no signs of habitation whatsoever. The only signs that Joe could see that anything at all lived here were the massacred bodies of unicorns and what appeared to be vampires. The snow surrounding these carcasses was an odd mixture of brown and red. This snow flurry was now escalating into a storm, and Joe could hardly see more than ten feet ahead of him.

And then the snow cleared, just like that. Joe could see a castle towering over the horizon. Then he saw two forms walking towards him. He wasn't trusting anything in this strange new world, so he turned and started to run but was stopped dead in his tracks by two new figures. He backed up and looked from side to side at the two approaching figures. Joe drew his sword and stopped.

On one side, Stephanie and Adrian walked towards him, Stephanie dressed in a black jumpsuit and Adrian in what looked like a ceremonial blue and green robe covered in tribal markings. On the other side, Adrian and Stephanie walked up to him, each wearing the same thing as the other two except in reverse. Joe opened his mouth to ask what was going on, but before he could make a sound...

"You bastard," the Stephanie in the black jumpsuit said. "I trusted you."

"What are you talking about?" Joe asked.

"Don't play dumb with us," the Adrian in the black jumpsuit said. "I can't believe we actually believed you." Joe looked at Adrian; he had no expression at all on his face. Stephanie on the other hand was in tears, but she made no sound. "All the time that you pretended to trust us..."

"That you pretended to be our friend..." Stephanie said. The both of them drew daggers from their pockets.

"You made us do this," they said in unison, and they threw the daggers. One lodged itself in the middle of Joe's chest, and the other slid easily into his back.

Joe's mouth dropped open and he gasped in pain. He staggered forward and fell face down in the snow, blood pooling around his stomach. The darkness swirled around and around him, and then it devoured him.

NINE

Joe is young again, thirteen years old and partially carefree. He is sitting in one of those green seats on a yellow school bus. Earphones placed comfortably in his ears, Joe is minding his own business. Then a piece of granola hits him in the back of the head. He looks up from the book that he is reading, but refrains from saying anything. He looks back to the book and continues reading. He is pelted with several more pieces of granola. Joe looks up again, but still refrains from saying anything. He returns to his book.

Once again, he is pelted with pieces of granola. Now he's mad. He drops the book, yanks the earphones out of his ears and stands up, turning around. He eyes the only two people (that he can see) behind him. The extremely obese Lanicia, and the sickeningly skinny Diamond. "Who's throwing those?" He asks through gritted teeth. The two of them look at each other, and then bust out laughing. Joe shakes his head and sits back down. He replaces his earphones, picks up the book and then thumbs through it until he finds the page that he was on. He continues reading.

He looks up in time to see Diamond move three seats ahead of him and start rummaging through her purse for something. Joe returns to his book. What happens next to this day humiliates Joe to think about. One moment he is reading his book, and the next, Lauriana (Lanicia's little sister) is pouring warm honey on his head, and Lanica is emptying a large bag of granola oats on him to complete the package. And then the honey and the granola oats stopped. He looks up and sees that Diamond has captured the entire thing on tape. Joe can feel the honey dripping off of his face and onto his new clothes. And then it comes. That horrible laughing. Everyone's laughing, even the bus driver. Over the laughter, he can hear Lanicia's high pitched voice shout out "Ha! Faggot ass bitch!" Then she continues laughing.

Joe is overwhelmed by anger now. He picks up his book bag and hurls it at Lanicia. She stops laughing. "Hold up. Who the fuck do you think you're throwing shit at?"

"I'm throwing it at the overly large dog that won't stop howling."

"Sit down!" The bus driver shouts. Neither one of them sits. Then the bus stops at Lanicia's stop. Without taking her eyes off Joe, she leans down (Joe can see the discomfort on her face), picks up her bag and jacket and

proceeds to the front of the bus. She reaches Joe, stares at him for a second, then speaks.

"Sit down," she pushes him down, drenching her hands in honey. "Bitch." She walks onward.

Joe picks up his book and hurls it at her. The book makes contact with the back of her gargantuan head. She turns around, ready to charge but Joe's two friends Stephanie (McDonald) and Zoe stand up to block her way.

"You think I'm scared of you two skinny bitches?"

"Get off the bus!" The bus driver shouts at her. She casts one final glance at Joe, and then gets off the bus.

Joe gathers up his belongings and returns to his seat, starting to become nauseous from the aroma of the honey. When the bus arrives at his stop five minutes later, he disembarks and walks slowly home. Once home, he showers and goes to bed early, refusing to tell anyone of his school bus ordeal. The next morning he awakes and has his mother drive him to school.

Once there, he enters the cafeteria as he normally does, and he's horrified to see Lanicia on stage next to the pull down screen. On the screen, is the video of him being doused in honey and granola oats, playing over and over again. And now, the entire middle school is laughing at him. His trust in the human race is shattered. Joe is humiliated and runs from the room before anyone sees that he entered in the first place. He stops outside the nurse's office to catch his breath, and then slowly makes his way to his favorite teacher's room.

"Joe, you're not supposed to be out of the cafeteria yet." The teacher says. Joe looks up at him, and begins to audibly sob.

"I don't know how much more I can take of this," Joe confesses.

"What happened?" And the two of them talked. They talked through the sounding of the bell, and throughout the rest of the day. The talking only stopped when the teacher needed to go up and talk to the class.

Joe respected this teacher, so he listened to every word that he said. And he allowed this teacher's words to shape him. This teacher was one of the last people that Joe opened up to. Before his two best friends and the large man named Aronus. And of course his two new "friends" who stab him in the back, just as the others did. (Only this time, much more literally).

When their talk ends at 3:00 that afternoon, the teacher invites him to stay the last forty minutes of the day. Then he asks if Joe is alright. Joe nods and says yes.

And he was.

TEN

Joe woke up in confusion. Directly in front of him, stood the Stephanie and Adrian in the black jumpsuits. Adrian held the sword firmly in his grasp. Joe's hands were chained above his head, his shirt was off, and there was some kind of *goop* covering up his wounds. He looked back up at the two people that he had started to call his friends. And behind them, was another Stephanie and another Adrian. The ones in the ceremonial green and blue robes covered in tribal markings.

"What's going on?" Joe asked, looking at the four of them Tears were streaming down Stephanie's face again. The two in the front refused to speak, so the two in the back did.

"You've hurt your last person." Adrian said.

"What—" Joe began, a look of pain and confusion spreading over his face.

"Oh, don't look at us like that," Stephanie said. "We tried to do this more subtle like."

"But to be perfectly honest… I'm getting a little tired of subtle."

"Exactly," Stephanie said. "Why should anyone be subtle with you?" You were never subtle with us." She smirked.

"What are you talking about?" Joe asked. And then his question was answered, because the both of them *changed*. Adrian shrunk and his skin became lighter. His hair grew out became red as it braided itself. Where the Adrian in the ceremonial robe had once stood, was now a short, chubby boy with red cornrows and acne beginning to set in. Stephanie's hair became longer and lighter. She also shrunk, and her facial features partially changed. In the place where the Stephanie in the ceremonial robe once stood, was now a short skinny girl.

"Aaron...Sarah...why?" The real Stephanie and Adrian turned around and backed away in horror. Joe's eyes glistened with tears as they threatened to spill over. These two people that Joe was looking at, these two runts who appeared to be stuck in time at age fourteen, used to be Joe's best friends in the world. The two that he loved and trusted more than anyone else in the world. And now they stood before him, apparently key figures in the plotting of his murder. Out of every heartbreak before, this was by far the worst. Joe had never hurt more than he hurt right now. And if he didn't know better, he would have sworn that he heard his heart shatter in his chest. The pain was certainly there. "I thought you were my friends."

"Friends?" Sarah asked sarcastically with a laugh. "We never liked you in the first place. I almost killed Aaron for giving you my number."

"But..."

"Why do you think I never stayed on the phone with you after Sarah hung up? And made up some excuse to get off when I did." Aaron was deadly serious as he said this. His voice was high, on the verge of deepening.

"You're a needy, bitchy, pathetic excuse for a person who can't take a hint. No one that you've ever considered a friend has liked you. Hell, *they* don't ever like you." Sarah pointed to Stephanie and Adrian.

"You tricked us!" Stephanie choked out.

"We just built on what was already there. The doubt, the mis-trust." Sarah said with a smirk. "It really wasn't that hard. You two are so gullible."

"Joe...We're so sorry," Stephanie said. "Can you ever forgive us?"

"We'll talk about this later." He said without taking his eyes off of his two former friends. "Why do this," he asked. "Why have two innocent people stab me and chain me up?"

"Because you don't *deserve* friends. You're a conceited asshole who doesn't care about anyone but yourself. You didn't give a damn about me or Aaron the entire time that we pretended to be your friends." And then Joe remembered it. All the pain and the loneliness that he felt. The nights that he would sit up waiting for the phone to ring like a pathetic little puppy dog. Now he understood. They never cared about him at all.

"You're right," Joe said. "I didn't deserve friends. I still don't. But at least I see these two more than once every six months."

"They're stuck with you," Aaron told him. "You're traveling an alien world. You're their only way home. Do you really think that they *want* to be walking around with you.

"You're pathetic," Sarah said. "The only people who can even stomach spending time with you are your parents. And they only do it because they have to."

"Really?" Joe asked. "Did you have to?" She looked at him, pursing her lips. "All those nights on the phone, you and Aaron telling me how much you care. Trying to stop me from doing whatever horrible thing I was planning? Did you have to do it Sarah?"

"I did it because—"

"You did it because you needed us. Just like we needed you." Joe said. He saw a tear fall from her eye. And let his go too. His voice broke as he spoke. "Sarah this isn't you. This isn't either of you. I thought the both of you were stronger than that. How could you let something creep inside of you and defile you like this? Humph! Shows how wrong I was."

Sarah fell over on her hands and knees and let out a gut-wrenching scream. A shadow shot forth from her mouth and up into the air. It floated there. Aaron looked up, eyes literally red with fury.

"Odesson you were always the weak one!" His voice was now deep and filled with rage.

"Her feelings," this voice came from the shadow. It too was deep, but not nearly as deep as whatever thing was possessing Aaron. "Huidon they're too powerful. I can't handle it."

"Obviously. Odesson you're weak. You've always been weak. And you've failed this order for the last time."

"Huidon please," the shadow called Odesson pleaded. "Have mercy. I'll try again."

"Too late." And his eyes glowed a brighter red. And then Odesson bellowed and caught fire, and then there was nothing. Aaron/Huidon looked back to Joe. "Now that my friend is gone, there's no reason to let your little friend live." He looked down at Sarah, still on her hands and knees. With lightning fast speed, he reached down, grabbed Sarah by the back of the neck, and held her up.

"No! Please, let her go." Aaron/Huidon looked at him, clearly puzzled.

"She would have killed you, given the chance." He said.

"That's because of your friend." Joe spat.

"No! There was already something there. Some hatred of you in her heart, or else he would have never been able to enter her. He merely capitalized upon the feelings and exploited them. And in the end, her feelings are what did him in. Whoda thought?" Then Joe looked behind him and saw Adrian with the sword, preparing to strike.

"Adrian, **NO!**"" Joe shouted, but it was too late. Adrian drove the sword through Aaron/Huidon. Now it was Aaron's turn to scream in blood-curdling agony. The shadow was expelled. Joe concentrated. "Evil shadow here, possessing ones held dear. No longer may you dwell, hell takes you with this spell."

Huidon's last words were "I'll be back!" And then he exploded. Aaron fell off of the sword and onto the ground.

"Cut me down," Joe said. "CUT ME DOWN!" Adrian cut him down. Joe ran over to Aaron where Sarah was already crouched over him, crying a river. "Aaron, please! Please, you have to get up! As the blood pooled around him, Adrian backed away, shaking his head. His face was frozen in an expression that said 'that didn't just happen. I didn't just do that.' He let the sword fall to the floor.

Sarah's words were barely comprehendible through her tears, but she spoke anyway. "Aaron baby please! Please wake up!" Her tears gathered around the wound. Then something miraculous happened. The tears entered the wound and the blood around his stomach receded. The wound healed and Aaron started to breathe again. Sarah looked up and smiled, wiping the tears away. Aaron turned himself over.

"This is the last time that I go on vacation with you." The three of them laughed. Then both Aaron and Sarah *changed* again. Aaron thinned up and became more muscular. His face aged and the acne that was beginning to set in vanished. Sarah blossomed. She grew taller and filled out more. And she was beautiful.

ELEVEN

The three of them talked for over an hour catching up. Aaron and Sarah apologized repeatedly for the ordeal that they had put him through. Then they parted. Joe insisted that they come along with him and his new friends, but they said that they had some things to finish up there. So Adrian and Stephanie led him back the way that they had come

"How come my wounds don't hurt?" Joe asked them halfway back to the portal.

"You know that stuff that was covering them up?" Stephanie asked. Joe nodded. "Well, it was meant to heal you. They said something about sacrificing you later on. Once you were better."

"Oh." Joe said. And the walked on.

They reached the portal and took one final glace around this winter world. Joe noticed something coming over the horizon, and then heard rumbling and shouting. In the other direction, Stephanie noticed the same thing. It was the vampires and the unicorns, waging one final battle to the finish. One species would reign supreme. The three of them jumped through the portal just as the two groups collided.

Then they were out again in that open field.

TWELVE

Joe grabbed the key that 214 had left behind, and then moved on. That night, while Joe slept, Adrian and Stephanie lay awake together, watching the stars. "I'm glad you're okay." He told her.

"What do you mean?"

"Once those two killed Joe, they would have come after us. And I don't know if I could bare it if something happened to you. I don't know what I'd do."

"Really?"

"Yeah." The two of them looked at each other, and then Adrian kissed her. They pulled apart after a couple of seconds, but their foreheads remained together. Adrian felt as though a tiny piece of him had been transferred into her. The two of them lay back, and spent the rest of the night watching the sky.

Made in the USA
Lexington, KY
02 June 2012